# LITTLE PARANOIAS: STORIES

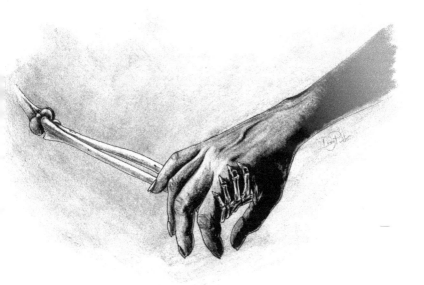

## BY SONORA TAYLOR

Little Paranoias: Stories by Sonora Taylor

For more information, visit the author's website at www.sonorawrites.com

This is a work of fiction. Names, characters, businesses, places, events and incidents are either the products of the author's imagination or used in a fictitious manner. Any resemblance to actual persons, living or dead, or actual events is purely coincidental.

Cover art by Doug Puller.

# TABLE OF CONTENTS

*To Sheri, whose friendship and help have been equally invaluable. I'm happy to know you.*

# LITTLE PARANOIAS

I worry what they'll do to me.
I worry what they'll say.
These little paranoias
Are what drive my day-to-day.

# WEARY BONES

Brandon sipped his tea as he watched TV. Occasionally, a gust of rain splashed against his house like water crashing from a thrown bucket; otherwise he paid no attention to the storm outside. He'd had a long day, one spent dusting and cleaning and tending to his wards. They were all asleep — as asleep as they could be — and now, he had an evening to himself.

He chose to spend that evening with *Law and Order: SVU*. Olivia Benson had long retired, and her great-granddaughter, Tiffany Benson-Sweet, had taken up the mantle of investigation. But through all the seasons and all the Bensons, Brandon still found the show to be a comfort after a long day at work.

His doorbell rang, a single chime that sounded over the television. Brandon sighed as he set down his mug and turned off the TV. So much for an evening to himself. He stood up and winced at his aching knees. He frowned at the sheets of rain unfurling outside of his window. Who would come to see him in this weather?

3

Brandon opened the door. A skeleton stood on his porch. It stood upright, its hollow eyes staring into Brandon's face. Rain ran down its skull and fell in droplets off of its ribs. Its teeth were clenched, and its arms hung slack by its sides.

Brandon nodded towards the living room. "Come on in," he said.

———

It started with a serum to ease the pain of death. It didn't prevent death, but promised a second life to people when their bodies stopped working. "Eventually, we hope to have a serum that gives people as many lives as cats," its inventor quipped on TV.

Dr. Soo Lin McCarthy watched the press conference from her lab and chewed on her fingernail. She wasn't as excited as her colleagues, for she knew what they meant by a second life. If it had been up to her, they wouldn't be presenting the serum at all. But it wasn't up to her, something their managers made clear despite the rattling in the rats' cages that could be heard even through closed doors. "It'll be fine once we get it to human testing," her managers assured her.

Soo Lin wasn't involved with human testing, but she gathered from the active silence about the effects of the serum that it hadn't been much better for them than it had been for the rats. She shuddered at the memory as the televised press conference continued and the serum's inventor announced patients would soon be able to request it at all medical offices.

She could still hear the sound of bone against metal, a clanking that had sounded like marbles spilling or dice rolling whenever she opened the door. She could still see the rats' eyeless faces staring at her, hungry for food they couldn't

4

eat. She could still feel the sickness in her stomach that grew with every crunch she'd heard when her bosses ordered the rats to be destroyed.

Soo Lin bit through her fingernail, then spit the nail into the trash. She turned off the TV and got her coat. People would find out soon enough how good the serum's promise was.

———————

Brandon didn't remember the promises of the doctors or the excitement in the papers. He barely remembered the pain of the serum. He'd received it when he was three, and all he remembered was the cool seat beneath his legs and the white walls he studied while a nurse promised him a lollipop.

What he remembered more was seeing his grandfather die. His grandfather was able to stay at home because of the serum, although he was bedridden in Brandon's earliest memories. On the night he took a turn for the worse, everyone gathered in his grandfather's room. Brandon stood restless next to his mother, and watched as his father stared at Brandon's grandfather. His Aunt Maria sobbed in the corner, and his Uncle Leo patted her shoulder. "He's going to come back," Leo said assuringly. "You don't have to cry."

"It's still sad," Brandon's father said with a frown, one Brandon usually saw when he spilled his cereal or told his father no. "She's allowed to grieve."

"And I'm allowed to comfort my wife," Leo shot back.

"Do you really need to do this now?" his mother snapped, as Aunt Maria cried harder.

They were all silenced by a deep, sudden breath. The family looked at the bed. Brandon's grandfather didn't move.

"Dad?" Brandon's father stepped toward his grandfather. Aunt Maria wiped her tears and leaned forward. Brandon still remembered the way his mother's fingers pressed into his shoulders as Brandon's father took his grandfather's hand.

"No pulse," his father said.

"How long does it take?" Aunt Maria asked.

"Do they have a pulse when they come back?" Uncle Leo added.

"Leo," Aunt Maria warned.

"What? I'm just wondering."

"Shit!"

Everyone looked at Brandon's father as he jumped back. His palm appeared to be melting, but Brandon realized the blood, ooze, and skin weren't his. They were his grandfather's. Brandon stood on tiptoe and watched in awe as his grandfather's body rippled and dripped, the skin dissolving and the blood congealing into the organs. His lungs, stomach, and other parts that Brandon didn't know the names of all began to beat like his heart. They beat as they dissolved, vanishing into the pool of bodily sludge that seeped into the sheets.

Aunt Maria screamed, while Uncle Leo turned to vomit into a small trashcan. Brandon's mother spun him out of the room just as his grandfather's heart faded into his ribs.

---

Meanwhile, in a small town almost a hundred miles away, Penny Pinkerton unknowingly thrust atop a dead man. "Come on, Glenn," she said as she lifted his hands to her hips. "Put some effort into it." She arched her back and jutted out her breasts, which she knew he loved and always responded to.

Glenn's hands slid down her waist. Penny opened her eyes and saw him lying still beneath her. He wasn't breathing, despite their chosen activity for the evening.

Penny slid off of him. It was his heart, maybe, or a stroke, or some other health problem that hadn't come up between them during any of their weekly visits at the Super 8. She wasn't about to spend a lot of time finding out. That would be for his wife to deal with.

The staff could also deal with moving the body. Penny covered Glenn with the comforter, then grabbed her coat from the chair and put it on over her pink lingerie. There was no point getting dressed at this hour, not even for the long drive in the cold back to her apartment. She'd been looking forward to a warm evening with Glenn.

She glanced back at the bed. Glenn was now a body under a blanket — a dirty hotel blanket at that. Penny could've sworn the stains that were already on it had grown since she'd covered him. The hotel's smell was also starting to get to her now that sex wasn't distracting her senses. Penny turned away with a sneer and walked towards the phone. It was time to do her part and get out.

"Hi," a lazy voice answered when she called the front desk. "How can I help you?"

Penny was about to say, "The man I'm with has died." But upon thinking the phrase, a lump formed in her throat. Glenn was dead. She wouldn't see him anymore, wouldn't be able to call him when she felt lonely, wouldn't drive to the Super 8 each Friday night and enjoy his company. Glenn was gone.

"Hello?" the front desk assistant asked.

"Hi. Yes." Penny spoke as well as she could with a choked voice.

"How can I help you?"

Penny took a deep breath. She refused to be sentimental about Glenn. She'd miss him, but he'd never been hers. He certainly wouldn't be now. She closed her eyes and allowed herself a few final memories, like how his lips had grazed her chin and how his palms had held her waist. She swore she felt his fingers touch her cheek.

A scratch along her ear broke her thoughts. She turned around and was face-to-face with a skull. A bony hand caressed her cheek.

Penny's scream sounded loud and clear through the phone.

———

Brandon's grandfather stayed in their house, despite the lingering fright from the transformation on his death bed. Whenever his grandfather walked from room to room, the creak of his bones sounding through the halls, Brandon's parents would exchange a wary glance.

Brandon, however, didn't mind. While his grandfather couldn't do everything he'd done before, like tell him bedtime stories or hold Brandon in his lap (he'd tried, but Brandon complained about the bumps on his butt), they could still play games or sit on the porch and watch the sunset.

Brandon especially loved playing games with dice. He liked the sound of the dice rattling in his grandfather's palms. His grandfather noticed, and always made sure to take his turn with extra flourish. He'd sometimes hold the dice up to his empty eye sockets, which always made Brandon laugh.

"How long can we keep a skeleton in the house, though?"

Brandon's parents spoke behind him while he watched TV, convinced he wasn't listening. His grandfather had already gone to bed. "It's been over a year," his father continued. "I loved Dad — I love Dad — but it's not Dad. It's just his bones."

"It is Grandpa," Brandon said as he turned around. "He plays with me and watches TV and —"

"It's a memory of Grandpa," his mother said.

"No, it's him! If it wasn't him, then why would he be moving around and playing games and —"

"It's not the same," his dad said. "And there's more to think about than keeping Grandpa's memory around the house."

"He's not a memory!" Brandon jumped up and stormed out of the room before his parents could say more. He ran up the stairs, then slowed his pace as he approached his grandfather's door. He almost felt a coolness coming from the other side of the door, like the feel of an autumn walk.

Brandon opened the door and saw his grandfather propped up in bed, reading a newspaper. Brandon wondered how he could still read, even without eyes. Maybe something in the serum brought back memories of words, or let him see through sockets instead of eyeballs.

His grandfather looked up at him. He waved and patted the mattress, turning the paper to reveal the comics. Brandon smiled as he joined his grandfather, who put an arm around Brandon's shoulders. Brandon read the panels out loud, and barely noticed the feel of bone against his back. He did see a white, dusty film across the pages, streaks left with every flick of his grandfather's fingers. Brandon's heart grew heavy as he realized his grandfather, like bones in a cemetery, would turn to dust. But they could read together before that happened.

———

It'd been hard enough for Marion to watch her child slowly die from cancer. Cecily had spent the last two years of her life in and out of the hospital. Tubes and beeping machines had become as prominent in Marion's memory as Cecily happily banging on the dashboard during drives, or the soft sound of her cries when she'd had a nightmare. Cecily was too young to be so sick, their time together too short. Cecily would never have a first day of school. She'd barely had a life outside of diapers. Even after the effects of the serum had become well known, Marion thought having her daughter back in some capacity would give them both the life together the disease had stolen from them.

Cecily had died at home, per Marion's request. She'd left Cecily sleeping in her bed and closed the door behind her so she wouldn't have to see the transformation. She'd already laid down a rubber sheet to catch the blood. As she waited in her room, she imagined hearing Cecily's cries once more, the whimper that meant Cecily would soon be crawling into bed with her after a nightmare.

Marion waited, then waited some more. Her eyes grew heavy, but she was startled awake by a loud rattle. It jangled and clanged down the hall, the sound of bone against a wooden door. Her daughter was back — but Marion felt a sickness in her stomach at the sound of bones.

She shook her head. Cecily was alive, and that was what mattered. She rose to her feet to go hug her daughter.

Marion could not grow used to the feel of Cecily's skeleton in her arms. Cecily longed to be held, longed to eat her favorite cereal and to play with Barbies. She could eat the cereal (though Marion refused to add milk), but Marion could barely eat as she watched Cecily's Lucky Charms fall down her rib cage. She'd play with Cecily and her Barbies, but Marion could only see a skeleton braiding Barbie's hair.

Looking at Cecily's skeleton reminded Marion of her death every time. Marion remembered the tubes, the beeps, the shallow breaths and endless rounds of vomiting. She remembered holding her daughter's hand in the hospital, her skin weak and her bones showing through more with each passing week.

Marion cried every night after Cecily crawled into bed. She thought the serum would give them both a second life. Cecily lived, but Marion perpetually grieved, reminded every day of the daughter she'd lost.

Marion first saw a commercial for the living cemeteries as she watched TV through teary eyes. Many people couldn't cope with the living memento mori of their loved ones, so cemeteries were now being used to house the skeletons. Caretakers watched them, and they were surrounded by other skeletons and the people who visited them.

She'd dismissed the notion, but with each passing day, she wasn't sure if she herself could live, so long as Cecily's bones clattered through the halls. She'd forever be in mourning, even when Cecily became nothing but dust. Skeletons were supposed to disappear in graveyards. Only memories were supposed to fade in houses.

They went for one last drive together. Marion fastened Cecily's seat belt, careful not to press the belt too tight against her ribs. Cecily banged on the dashboard like she had as a girl. Marion tried not to tense at the sound of bone hitting vinyl. "Stop, honey," Marion said as she gently took Cecily's hand.

Cecily stopped, and curled her fingers around her mother's palm. Marion blinked back tears, but not at the feel of bone.

For the rest of their drive to the cemetery, all she felt was the warm skin of her daughter's hand.

———

Brandon didn't mind the living cemeteries at all. He often waved at the skeletons when he walked by on his way to and from school. Sometimes they waved back. Other times, they nodded in his direction.

Most passersby turned their heads, but Brandon wasn't the only one who waved. There were others like him who didn't mind the bones, who saw them as a regular part of their lives, not creepy reminders of the people they'd lost.

Whatever one's thoughts on the bones, there were more and more of them every day — and with more skeletons came more crowding, more grime, and more concern. People may have been uncomfortable keeping their loved ones in their home, but they didn't want their loved ones' care to fall to the wayside.

As such, their care within the living cemeteries became a bigger priority. As Brandon walked by the cemetery on his usual route, he saw a flyer taped to the iron gate:

*Help Wanted: Caretaker(s) to help with skeletons. Tasks: clean dirt and grass from bones, clean grave beds, interact with residents, etc.*

Brandon thought of his grandfather, who'd perished long before the living cemeteries were in place. His bones had worn to shells that Brandon had feared would become ash at any moment. They sat on the porch, and Brandon noticed his grandfather hadn't moved in some time. When he studied his grandfather, he swore he saw contentment deep within the hollow of his face — a contentment Brandon felt surely came from not being alone when he'd passed.

It was nothing like the feeling he got when he walked by the cemetery. Clustered together, the skeletons emanated waves of sadness that Brandon could feel. They were being forgotten while the living moved on.

These skeletons were alone. Even clustered against one another in cemeteries, and seen by friends and family who dared to visit them, they slept and woke up alone. They were left to wither away above ground. Brandon couldn't stop them from withering, but he could lessen their loneliness during the process.

"Can I help you, young man?" Brandon looked up and saw an older woman approach the gate. "You here to visit someone, or —"

"I'm reading about the caretakers," Brandon said. "Do you hire high schoolers?"

---

Mandy hated walking home after work. The route was safe, and there was never any trouble. The sidewalks were awash in light from the streetlamps, and the empty office buildings lining them shimmered with lit windows. Still, she walked down the sidewalk wary of the darkened corners, head up high and hands in her pockets.

What creeped her out the most was the living cemetery. It'd been creepy enough when it was just a regular cemetery, silent graves that seemed to watch her as she passed by. It got worse when all the skeletons were crowded into it. Most were still when she walked by them, resting in some form of sleep. How did they sleep? Did they just turn off when the sun went down?

However they did it, they creeped Mandy the hell out. She braced herself as she rounded the corner, prepared for the view of a sea of bones lined up one-by-one, the path of ribs almost creating a wave that rippled through the night.

She was greeted by an empty cemetery, filled only with stones.

Mandy stopped and stared. Where had the skeletons gone? Were the caretakers cleaning them? Had they been moved somewhere out of sight?

For the sake of her nightly walk, Mandy hoped they'd been moved. She continued past the graveyard and moved down the sidewalk. The wind was cold on her cheeks. She wanted to get home, change out of her waitressing uniform, and have a cup of tea.

A loud, sickening crack burst behind her. Mandy jumped, then turned around. She saw no one there, no broken trees or shattered rock.

She looked down, and saw a pile of bones at her feet. A skull lay on a bed of broken ribs and femurs. Its mouth and eyes gaped up at her, seeming to ask questions in response to her own.

Another crack sounded behind her. Mandy swiveled and saw another pile of bones, this one splayed in a line from the skeleton's shattered toes to its fractured head. "What the fuck?" Mandy whispered.

In answer, a skeleton fell from the sky a little further down the sidewalk. She watched it explode, its bones careening to all sides like shrapnel. She stepped back and felt a crunch beneath her feet. She saw a broken hand beneath her shoe, and felt a little nausea replace the fear that had settled in her stomach.

The sound of cracks came faster now, and on both sides of the street. Mandy looked up.

Skeletons lined the rooftops of the adjacent buildings. One by one, they jumped from the roofs and shattered on the sidewalks, their bones scattering across the pavement and concrete. Mandy ran into the middle of the street, moving as fast as she could so she wouldn't be hit. Her vomit landed on the pavement when she opened her mouth to scream.

––––––––––

So many were dead. If they weren't in pieces on the street, they had buried themselves under mud and sand, waiting for the water to wash them away more quickly than air ever could. Brandon scowled as he picked wet leaves off the skull of one of the only survivors of the Second Death, as the papers called the sudden rash of skeletons ending their reincarnation earlier than science intended.

It was all so unnecessary. It'd been over twenty years since the serum was introduced. The second chance at life was a part of everyone's life. So many people had gotten the serum that, even when it went off the market, people knew there would be skeletons for decades.

Why couldn't they accept that? Why did they have to shudder at the sight of the future that lay ahead for them all? Why did they have to shove those who lived again into places of the dead, like cemeteries and morgues? They were meant to hold those who were gone, those who couldn't feel or see. Those who would fade into the earth the same way they'd fade in their loved ones' memories.

"It's all so fucked up," Brandon said.

He'd spoken to himself, but the skeleton he tended to nodded. Brandon smiled.

"You don't like it here, do you?" Brandon asked.

The skeleton lifted its shoulder bones towards its chin in a makeshift shrug. There was a clatter when the shoulder bones dropped, as if its body rang with the defeat it felt at not knowing the answer.

"Where would you live — you know, if you could?"

Brandon realized he needed to think of a way to phrase the question as yes-or-no, but the skeleton turned before he could. The skeleton gathered some twigs and branches off the ground and wrote, in broken but discernible letters, *HOUSE*.

Brandon nodded. A house would be nice. So many houses, though, were owned by people who didn't want skeletons inside of them. If more people were like him and the other caretakers, perhaps the skeletons would have a home.

Brandon thought for a moment. Why couldn't he and the other caretakers bring the skeletons home? They'd be protected from the elements, and with people who weren't afraid of them. They could live out their lives, if not at home, then at least in a house with creature comforts. They would no longer be surrounded by the terrified eyes of passersby or reminders that they were still considered dead. They wouldn't feel compelled to jump, be buried, or be washed away. They would be home.

So, Brandon took them home.

———

Emily still thought of him sometimes. She thought of the way his brown hair hung in his face while he wiped dirt and leaves from a skull, how his clothes were often covered in bone dust and he'd wipe them from his jacket like a baker brushing flour from an apron. "Careful with the dust," she said one day. "I don't want to sneeze out someone's mother."

He'd looked up in surprise, and when he saw Emily's smile, he'd smiled as well. She held out her hand. "I'm Emily," she said. "I just started working in this cemetery."

"Brandon," he said as he shook her hand. "I've been working here for over five years."

"Wow. Guess this isn't part time for you, huh?"

"Not anymore. Why? Is this a summer job for you?"

The way Brandon's brow furrowed in spite of his smile should've told Emily that unless she saw a future in the graveyard, she'd have no future with him. In that moment, though, Emily only saw beautiful hazel eyes that held secrets. She wanted to uncover those secrets.

"At the moment, yeah," she replied. "Can't do full-time while I'm in school."

"High school?" Brandon asked.

"College."

He nodded and brushed back his bangs, a movement whose magic Emily couldn't deny. "Well, let me know if you need any help," he said as he turned to leave. "I'm here almost every day."

"Even on weekends?" Emily asked. "You don't go out for dinner or anything?"

She grinned and hoped he'd take the hint, but Brandon only shook his head.

"The work doesn't end," he said. "I'm here every day."

17

He left. Emily shrugged. "I mean, everyone's gotta eat," she muttered as she stooped to clean the hands of a skeleton with moss and dirt on its fingers.

The skeleton nodded, then placed its palm against its forehead before pointing in Brandon's direction. Emily chuckled a little. "Maybe he'd go if you told him to," she said.

Though he didn't seem interested in dinner, Brandon did seem more interested in her the longer she worked at the cemetery. He often worked close to her assigned corners, and offered to do her rounds with her when he wasn't busy. Emily felt her fleeting attraction root into something more palpable each day. She hoped, and searched for hints in his eyes or his smile that his thoughts had shifted from his work to her.

As weeks turned to months, and months into years, Emily knew that things between them would always be the same. Brandon wasn't interested. Emily was second to the dead.

She left her work in the cemetery upon graduation. She and Brandon promised to keep in touch, but she knew they never would.

When the Second Death occurred, she thought momentarily of the skeletons she'd cared for years ago. Mostly, though, she thought of Brandon. She thought of the way he cared for the skeletons as if they were all his deceased relatives. She thought of how he was probably mourning them, these skeletons who'd decided that total death was better than a partial life. She went to sleep that night hoping that he had someone who could comfort him.

———

Brandon's house became a destination for the local dead. He heard word of other caretakers following his example, but there were days when Brandon saw all the bones in his house and doubted that.

The other caretakers didn't matter, though. What mattered to Brandon was helping them. His grandfather had died with family both times. When his own parents died, they could come live with him too.

It was possible that it would be the only way he'd see them. They constantly asked Brandon to come see them, but wouldn't visit him. His mother still shuddered when she spoke of the bones. His father avoided the subject. His own mother and father were just like everyone else, the family, friends, and lovers who withdrew from him as his job expanded and his calling came through like a song.

Brandon spent more time at home, and more time with the skeletons and his television for company. If people didn't want to see the memento mori he cared for, the skeletons who just wanted some sort of connection to the life they'd been promised by the serum, then that meant they wouldn't see him either.

The years went by. The skeletons became his life — and for Brandon at least, it was a life well-lived.

———

Emily moved on in most every sense. She married, she had children and grandchildren. She grew old, and spent her afternoons on the porch looking out at the sky. She didn't know when death would come for her, but she was slightly comforted by the thought that when it came, that would be the end. She'd been born after the serum had revealed itself to everyone, and never received it. She wouldn't become a walking reminder that she had already died, ignored or avoided by those who wouldn't, or couldn't, mourn the dead among them forever. Those who weren't like Brandon.

She hadn't thought of his name in years, and yet when it flickered in her mind, she saw him standing in the graveyard brushing dirt and bone dust from his palms. She wondered if he was alone. She wondered if he'd turned into one of his beloved skeletons. Did he still care for them as they dwindled in number, the cemeteries once again becoming places for bodies, and the memories they carried, to be buried in the ground?

Emily looked at her wrinkled hands. They'd grown so thin that one could almost see the bones inside of them. She smiled a little as she took in her skeletal appearance. Maybe now, Brandon would be willing to hold her hand.

---

"Do you want a cup of tea?"

In lieu of furrowing its absent brow, the skeleton pointed to its throat and then the gaps in its ribs.

"I know," Brandon said. "It was a joke — granted, not a very good one."

The skeleton stood still. Brandon sighed a little. He turned away, then heard a faint rattle. He looked back at the skeleton. It nodded its head and opened its mouth, so it looked more like it had a smile. Its hands were on its ribs, which shook up and down. The bones rattled, and in their clacking, Brandon could almost hear the *ha ha ha*.

Brandon chuckled and turned back toward the kitchen.

"Well, feel free to have a seat," he said as he walked to the stove. "I'm just going to have another cup, and then —"

A violent pang shot up his leg. Brandon swiveled and grabbed his knee, but the turn sent him spiraling. As he fell towards the hard linoleum floor, Brandon wondered what it was like for his wards, who saw and heard and felt despite their lack of bodies. Were their senses like memories, flickers in their skull that helped them move through the next phase of life? He supposed he was about to find out.

Brandon's back fell against a hard bar, one that splintered beneath him. Brandon felt fingers grip his waist. The bar pushed him upward, and Brandon realized that it was a bone.

The skeleton had broken his fall. The skeleton had saved him from death — or at the very least, a score of fractures and breaks that would've rendered Brandon immobile.

The skeleton cradled him as it helped him to his feet. It used both hands to steady Brandon before gently lifting its fingers away to see if Brandon could stand. He stood still, and stared into the skeleton's hollow eyes. He stared death in the face — and yet, this death that others avoided while they were alive had kept him living for a while longer.

"Thank you," Brandon said.

The skeleton gave a single nod.

"Come on — I'll get you to an empty room." Brandon nodded towards the stairs. Though he was careful to not move too fast, he walked delicately to ease his aching knees and, now, his sore legs and hip. He trembled — just a little, but enough for the skeleton to wrap its arm around his waist. Brandon was about to shake it off, but stopped. He allowed his weary body to be guided by weary bones, both of them ready to rest.

# NEVER WALK ALONE

Jordan walked home with a bit of fear. She wasn't afraid of the dark, or even her neighborhood. She was more afraid that her walk home would be disrupted in a way that would validate everyone who'd told her to never walk alone.

She frowned as she remembered the voices of teachers, counselors, and her parents warning her about the dangers that lurked around every corner. Her boyfriend Kyle had been the worst. He hovered over her every move when they were together, and there were times she wanted nothing more than to swat him away like a gnat.

A mosquito buzzed in her ear. Jordan smacked it and cursed at the ooze on her temple. Home — she had to get home. No distractions.

She walked along the darkened street. At times it was so quiet that her mind created the sound of footsteps by her side. But whenever she looked, no one was there.

Jordan turned the corner and smiled as she walked onto her street. She was almost home.

Jordan saw another shadow in the streetlight. She turned for a moment and saw someone walking behind her. She took a breath. She wouldn't clench her hands or stuff them into her pockets. She didn't want whoever was behind her to suspect she was afraid. She kept her eyes forward as she walked.

The footsteps drew closer. Jordan swore they were right on her heels.

She could hear change jingling in their pocket, and breathing that sounded in time with their steps. Jordan closed her eyes. How much closer would they get? How much of her could they clearly make out beneath the streetlight?

The person walked into the street and into Jordan's peripheral vision. She waited to see if they'd approach her.

The person turned down the block to their left, then disappeared.

Jordan smiled. She'd been left alone — no distractions. Walking home alone was fine, no matter what Kyle thought. She laughed a little, recalling Kyle's panic, but then she thought of all the times he'd yelled at her to not walk home alone. How he'd gone so far as to grab her shoulders that night to try and stop her.

Jordan's shoulders settled as she reached her home. Her journey was done, and she'd made it without anyone seeing her. She walked to the backyard and picked up the hose. She needed to wash Kyle's blood off of her hands before she went inside.

# A PART OF YOU

Travis and Tristan looked at their mother, dead on the floor. They grinned at the sight.

"That was easy," Travis said.

"Dad'll be thrilled," Tristan added. "He was right — the tea got her in just one sip."

"Let's go tell him. He'll be proud of us for —"

Travis stopped and stared at Tristan. Tristan stood frozen except for the blood seeping from his eyes like thin red threads spooling from each iris. Tristan's mouth fell open, and a stream of blood joined the trickles from his eyes.

Travis began to scream, then felt his stomach burst. He grabbed his belly, but instead of flesh, he grabbed bone. He looked down and saw two skeleton arms shoot from his stomach. They swatted his hands away like flies.

Before he could scream again, something else burst from his throat. He felt a large, smooth orb move from his neck. The skull cast a glance in his direction, then turned and dove towards the blood falling from Tristan's body. The hands cupped the blood and the skull began to sip. Skin and hair grew around the bones. Before Travis lost consciousness, he saw his mother's chestnut hair curl over her reborn shoulders.

"You can't kill me," she said to the lifeless forms of her sons. "You came from me, and I'm a part of you — one you'll never be able to destroy." She grabbed her tepid mug of tea and walked out of the kitchen. "Now, let's see where your father is."

# CRUST

The crust was Millie's least favorite part to make. She sighed as she ran her rolling pin over the stiff disk of dough. It needed to be cold for the butter to make it flaky, but it had to be warmer for her to roll it out. But she couldn't roll it out too thin, or else the crust would tear. And not too thick, or else it wouldn't be a crust at all.

Millie hated making her own crust, but that was the way her mother liked it. Homemade — nothing from a can or freezer. "You can't make everything easily," her mother would say as she spit a piece of pie into her napkin, Millie's latest effort an apparent failure. "You're spoiled, and that spoils your food."

Millie would swallow back her tears — "Tears just show how much you think you deserve sympathy," her mother would say, "and sympathy is earned" — and try again another week. She'd try and try, stirring the blueberries into a perfect compote, simmering the apples in sugar until they became thick and soft, baking the pumpkin puree until it formed into

27

a perfect, stable custard that didn't fall or seep, just wiggle a little. Millie was excellent at filling. It was just the damn crust.

She thrust the rolling pin too hard and tore the crust. "Dammit!" she yelled as she pressed the dough back together. She felt it warm beneath her fingers, felt the butter melt inside the flour before it had a chance to melt in the oven. It'd be less flaky now. It wouldn't be perfect. Millie threw the crust away, then turned to face her mother at the table.

"I won't make it if it isn't perfect!" she said as she blinked back tears. "I'll start over. Is that good enough for you?"

Her mother didn't reply. Her mother hadn't said a word for weeks, not since she'd died at the table while finishing her dinner. Millie had found her after placing another pie in the oven, sitting still, her mouth hanging open and her eyes vacant yet narrow.

She still sat there, her body crumbling like an oat topping, her skin wrinkled like an apple perfect for filling. Her eyes were dark and rotted, but Millie could still see the judgment within them. Eternally in disapproval, even though she couldn't voice it.

Millie could hear it in her head, though. "I'll make it better," she said as she turned to the fridge to get some butter. "I'll make it perfect."

# THE NOTE ON
# THE DOOR

Rory walked by the same door every day on her way to work. She walked by many homes with many doors, but on Monday morning, only one caught her eye — one with a note taped to the glass.

Rory kept walking. Walking up to a stranger's porch to read another stranger's note would make her look like a creep in front of her fellow commuters.

Tuesday and Wednesday went by in time with her steps. The note remained on the door.

On Thursday, she stopped and tried to read it from the sidewalk. She could see handwritten scrawl, but not what it said. She turned and walked away. The note wasn't written for her.

On Friday, she could no longer bear it. She glanced from side to side to make sure no one would see her trespass. She walked up the porch and to the door. She read the note:

*If you're reading this, please help me! The key is under the vase.*

Rory shivered as she looked for the key. If only she'd read the note sooner. She found the key and almost dropped it twice as she unlocked the door. She stepped inside and saw five red lines on the wall, ending abruptly with a smeared, bloody palm print.

Rory dropped the key and sighed. She was too late.

A hand clasped her throat. Rory felt warm breath on her ear and a body press against her. Her heart raced. "Thanks for reading my note," a man's voice whispered.

Rory's excitement grew as she reached into her tote bag. In one swift motion, she pulled out her knife and plunged it into the leg of the man behind her. He dropped to the floor and cried out in pain.

"No," she said with a smile as she turned to face the man. "Thank you for writing it."

# ALWAYS IN MY EAR

Brooke walked down the street and fiddled with the golden beetle in her ear. It was brand new, a replacement for the silver beetle that had only come out weeks before. The golden beetle promised a month's worth of podcasts before it needed to recharge, and audio so clear it seemed like a whisper from a lover, even on a crowded street.

A month of battery time was generous, and the promise of intimacy moreso. But Brooke could hear Victoria loud and clear as she purred her latest instruction: "Head to the park and look for a small pond. The one where all the fireflies glow."

Brooke rolled her eyes. There weren't any fireflies in Briar Park, not with winter around the corner. But Vicki's loyal listeners would love the puzzle — and Brooke would know where to look. It was the pond where they'd caught fireflies together after dark. Victoria knew that Brooke knew that. Brooke wondered if Victoria knew she was listening.

But to the rest of Vicki's listeners, all Vicki was doing was giving her best guess as to the whereabouts of a local killer.

Everyone's beetles buzzed with true-crime podcasts, where hosts talked about grisly murders and the criminals who committed them. Many of the hosts fancied themselves to be amateur detectives. Audiences were all too keen to become volunteer co-detectives, to have a portable alert that fed them theories, conspiracies, and history on Hollingsworth, Virginia's most notorious cold cases — the largest of all being a mysterious killer who'd killed four and possibly more in the past four years, and no suspect to show for the police's supposed work.

Few podcasts were as popular as *Vicki's Vigilantes*. Vicki hit the scene shortly after the anxiety about the murders in Hollingsworth hit a fever pitch, and after the beetles became a common appearance in people's ears. Her podcast actively guided people to suspects, and while she didn't say outright to kill them, her biggest fans — who called themselves the Vigil — were known for taking matters into their own hands.

Brooke knew that *Vicki's Vigilantes*, with its puzzles, popularity, and resulting kills throughout the city, was Victoria's proudest work. For while everyone thought they were solving cold cases, Brooke knew that Victoria was guiding her listeners to kill people who may or may not have killed anyone. She had simply created a game to destroy people. Murder was Victoria's favorite pastime, and back when they'd been friends, Victoria and Brooke had been Hollingsworth's most prolific serial killers.

———

Before they were murderers, they had been friends. They met by the pond in Briar Park, and bonded over things that little girls bond over: proximity, shared toys, and favorite shows and movies.

What they bonded over the most, though, were secrets. "Psst," Victoria said one day as they played by the pond.

Brooke looked at her curiously. Victoria beckoned Brooke with her finger. "What?" Brooke asked.

"I wanna tell you a secret."

"No one else is around."

"Doesn't matter. You have to whisper secrets. That way they always stay in your ear, and not in the air where they can fly and spread around."

Brooke smiled, charmed by the thought of a secret zipping through the wind like a glittery moth, with red eyes and white crystal teeth to match its wings. She walked closer to Victoria. "What is it?" she whispered.

Victoria cupped Brooke's ear and told her their very first secret: "There's a monster at the bottom of the lake."

Brooke frowned. "That's a lie. Secrets aren't supposed to be lies."

"How do you know it's a lie?"

"Because monsters aren't real."

Victoria grinned, then leaned close to Brooke again so she could whisper in her ear. "It's a toy monster. It belonged to Tommy, that mean kid in our class."

Brooke leaned back. "The one who —" But she stopped herself, and leaned back towards Victoria's ear. "The one who threw gum in your hair?"

"Yeah. I stole his toy and threw it in the pond. He still doesn't know where it is."

"That was his favorite toy."

Victoria lifted a lock of her slightly-shortened hair. "This is my favorite hair."

They began to giggle. "You should tell him it's there," Brooke said. "His monster's at the bottom getting eaten by fish."

"No, the monster's living under the sea," Victoria added. "Maybe Tommy will dive in after him."

"Maybe Tommy will drown while he looks for him."

"Let's hope so!" They laughed and laughed, happy to have found a place for each other's deepest secrets.

————

As they grew and came to know themselves, Brooke found she liked what Victoria liked. Victoria knew what Brooke knew. Both of them liked, and knew, darkness — darkness they could share with a whisper in the other's ear.

"Have you ever thought about what it'd be like to watch someone die?" Victoria asked one night. They were camping in a tent in Brooke's backyard.

Brooke looked from side to side, even though they were alone. She scooted closer to Victoria, who smiled when she realized Brooke was about to tell her a secret. She leaned in close as Brooke cupped her ear.

"I've seen someone die," Brooke whispered.

Victoria's eyes widened, but less in surprise and more in betrayal. "You never told me that. When?"

It'd been almost a year ago, the night before her thirteenth birthday. Brooke had tried to forget it, but the image kept appearing in her mind — and Victoria was the perfect person to share it with. "I was walking home," Brooke said.

"Someone grabbed my ankle. I yanked it away and saw a guy bleeding on the street."

"Was he shot?"

"Stabbed, I think. He bled all over. He whispered for help, but couldn't move."

"What'd you do?"

"I stared at him. I didn't move. I …" Brooke closed her eyes.

"You let him die." Brooke opened her eyes again, curious what Victoria thought. Victoria looked at her with intensity, but Brooke didn't see judgment or fear.

"I watched him die," Brooke whispered. "I wanted to watch him. I wanted to see what it was like."

"You can watch videos online. I heard about this site, where they've got videos with real victims, not the fake stuff you see in horror movies."

"It's not the same. I wanted to see it in person, and I felt less bad about it being an accident and not —"

"Done by you?"

Brooke's eyes widened. She looked down.

"How'd it feel?" Victoria asked.

Brooke kept her eyes down, but a small smile crept across her face. "It was cool," she said. "I could almost feel his soul dash from his body, like it was a secret that had been set loose."

"I bet it'd be even cooler if you set it loose yourself."

Brooke looked back up. Victoria had a mischievous smile, one Brooke recognized from all the times they'd shared secrets and hatched plans. This new plan, a darker plan, would take longer to incubate. But something told Brooke that this wouldn't just be talk inside their tent.

———

Brooke and Victoria continued their conversation for years through hushed secrets and elaborate planning. Brooke told herself the planning was pretend, even as their whispered imaginings grew darker and fluttered in her brain like vicious lunar moths.

Victoria would often ask her when they could set their planning free. "It'd be so much more fun to do it than talk about it, wouldn't it?" she asked one night as they sat by the pond. They could talk in secrecy without whispering in each other's ear, though Brooke still wondered sometimes if their words could hang in the air or glisten in the pond like the reflection of the moon.

"Maybe, but then it'd be out there," Brooke replied. "It wouldn't be our secret anymore."

"It could still be our secret. No one would know except the person dying. Don't you want to feel what you felt when you saw that man die? We can make it happen."

"I'm …"

"What is it?" Victoria leaned closer to Brooke. "Whisper it to me."

Brooke knew a whisper wouldn't make her feel less ashamed, but maybe it would help to know that it'd stay trapped in Victoria's ear. "I just — our secrets live in our ears," she whispered. "I know it's childish, but it's a thought that comforts me, knowing they have a home that's not just my own head. But I'm worried about what'll happen if we let them out."

Victoria leaned back, and Brooke wondered if she'd disappointed her friend. Victoria smiled a little as she nodded. "I get it. All our secrets are flitting around in each other's heads, like fireflies in jars."

"Yeah. Exactly."

"They're glowing and flying in their little glass case. They're trying to escape the jar, but they're under a lid."

"Right. Like the fireflies we used to catch." Brooke smiled. "Remember when we didn't even poke air holes, how they fell and crumpled one-by-one while we watched?"

"And that's what's happening to our secrets," Victoria said. "They won't get to fly and glow and become our goals. They'll just die inside our ears."

Brooke hadn't considered that. Her darkest secrets often rammed at her head, but she felt comforted when they transferred over to Victoria's mind. She didn't think that they were suffocating in the shared space of their imaginations.

"Think about it," Victoria said. "I won't do anything without you, but think about what we could do if we acted instead of whispered. Think about how you'd feel."

Brooke thought about it throughout her senior year. She thought so much that she would get lost during class, looking out the window and only seeing an imaginary someone bleed into the grass while she watched.

On graduation day, Brooke and Victoria stood in the hallway before they were separated by last name. She leaned to Victoria and whispered, "I've thought about it — and I don't want to just think anymore."

"A through E over here, F through K over here," the principal said, dividing Brooke and Victoria along with the other students. Victoria smiled at Brooke before they were shuffled apart.

That night, they celebrated in a bar with fake IDs. Brooke didn't think about their secrets, just the pleasant warmth of the beer softening her thoughts and muscles. She danced and she drank; she smiled and anticipated the future.

A finger tapping on her shoulder broke her reverie. Brooke turned, slightly annoyed, and grew even more so when she saw an inebriated man leaning against Victoria. "This is my friend I was telling you about," Victoria shouted. "Brooke, this is Carl."

"Hey Brooke," Carl slurred. "Your friend here tells me you'd be up for some fun tonight."

"I don't think so," Brooke said.

"Come on, don't you want to celebrate your graduation in style?" Carl asked.

"I thought we'd take him to the pond," Victoria added. "The one that no one goes to."

"You mean the one that no one went to," Brooke said, angry that their secret had been betrayed.

"You all got a secret pond?" Carl asked. "Is it like a fort or something?"

"It's just a pond in the woods out past the park." Victoria winked at Brooke before she could correct her and say it was in the park. "It's where we like to watch the fireflies."

Understanding dawned on Brooke. Carl leaned more heavily on Victoria. "Sounds like a perfect spot," he said as he looked at her cleavage.

"Yes," Brooke said as she slipped her arm around Carl's waist. "It is."

––––––––

Brooke and Victoria took turns stabbing Carl, then watched him bleed into the dirt as his screams became gurgled moans, then silence. Brooke felt the chill she'd felt when she'd first seen someone die, but she knew it wasn't his soul. It was something entirely hers, a rush that coursed through her blood — one she wanted to feel again and again.

Still, Brooke knew they had to be careful. "We have to plan," Brooke said as they buried Carl deep in the woods. "We have to be careful to not form a pattern."

"I know," Victoria said. She kicked dirt over his body. "We'll keep it to ourselves."

She stooped down next to Brooke and leaned close to her face. "We'll keep it in our ears," she whispered.

Brooke smiled, then leaned close and whispered back, "Along with their screams."

———

They agreed to celebrate the anniversary of their first kill with a new one, a solid year to keep them distanced. Enough time for the fireflies in Brooke's imagination to ram and glow, but not so long that she would feel them die in the folds of her brain.

The secrecy, though, seemed less important to keep the second time — at least in Victoria's mind. "What are you doing?" Brooke asked as Victoria snapped a photo of the body with her phone.

"Commemorating the occasion," Victoria said. "Don't you want to remember this?"

"Delete it."

"Come on, I'm not going to post it online — even if some snuff groups would pay a fortune for this."

Brooke rolled her eyes and stabbed their victim one last time. She turned and saw that Victoria had thankfully put her phone away. Even if Victoria never shared it, Brooke didn't trust that the photo would be safe. It would get out somehow. It existed outside of their own eyes and ears, in a device connected to the world. Brooke began to wonder just how much Victoria's phone could hear.

"Maybe don't bring your phone at all next time," Brooke said as they cleaned themselves up.

Victoria pressed her lips, the first flash of anger Brooke had seen in all their years of friendship. "I won't take any more pictures, Brooke."

"It could pick things up, listen to us —"

"Listen to us what? Stabbing people?"

"Shut up!"

Victoria rolled her eyes, but lowered her voice. "Don't get so worked up," Victoria said. "This is still our secret."

Brooke nodded. It was theirs and only theirs — but she wondered how much longer that would be.

———

Brooke and Victoria were good at covering their tracks, but that didn't stop the citizens of Hollingsworth from noticing that two of their brethren were gone. Police assured the public they were on the case, but with the fear of a killer on the loose combined with the rising interest of both true crime and visceral content fans, many people frequented online spaces looking for the latest grisly news to sate their appetites.

Victoria was eager to throw them a bone. "It'll be a game," Victoria insisted as she and Brooke washed their hands and knives after their third kill. "We can post anonymously —"

"Nothing's anonymous online."

"We'll find a way to mask ourselves. My cousin's in IT — maybe she can help."

"What are we going to tell her? That we need a great way to brag about killing people, but without leaving a digital footprint?"

"We can make something up! You know how many true-crime podcasts there are now? We can just say we're starting one or some shit like that."

"This isn't about getting clicks, though. It's about watching people die. It's about sharing something and getting it out of our heads —"

"But it can be more. It can get even bigger, maybe even bring us more victims."

Brooke didn't need more — and she was insulted by Victoria wanting more than what they already had. She pursed her lips and looked away from her.

"No," Brooke said. "End of discussion."

Victoria shook her head, but didn't continue to argue. She dropped it to keep the peace, but Brooke knew that peace was only temporary.

———

As the year went on, Victoria became preoccupied with murder sites and criminal podcasts. Rather than plan things for their fourth kill, like new places to hide the body, Victoria began to tell Brooke about podcasts to listen to. "Check this one out," she said for the umpteenth time as she turned her laptop to face Brooke. "It's about —"

"I'm not interested." Brooke hated the true crime podcasts. It was just people talking about murder instead of doing it, or else drooling over serial killers like they were pinups. Brooke's work wasn't meant to be worshipped. It was meant to be an accomplishment, something for her and Victoria alone to enjoy.

Brooke was more concerned with press coverage of what had been dubbed the Hollingsworth Murders. The police seemed no closer to pinpointing her and Victoria, but Victoria's obsession with true crime podcasts — and ways they could be featured on them — would make their being caught a greater possibility.

Still, they stayed friends who met up on Friday nights for movies and wine, who commiserated about their jobs over coffee, who planned the where and when of the fourth kill. Brooke tolerated Victoria's passion for the podcasts so long as they still spent time alone together. When they met on the night of their fourth kill, Brooke was pleased to see no outline of a phone in Victoria's pocket. She'd left it and its podcasts at home.

As they rolled their fourth body into the river, though, Brooke saw a shiny flash of bronze that told her she'd thought wrong. "What's that?" Brooke asked as she pointed at Victoria's ear.

"What's what?" Victoria asked. She brushed her hair over her left ear as she did so, which told Brooke that she knew exactly what. It was the latest device, an implant that allowed voracious podcast listeners to keep up with their favorite programs at all times.

"Is that a fucking beetle?" Brooke spat.

Victoria looked away, and Brooke marched to Victoria's left side. She saw two red dots blinking one after the other, like eyes peering at her from beneath Victoria's hair. "Is the beetle on right now?" Brooke asked.

"It's always on," Victoria said. "You know that."

"Why the fuck are you wearing one right now?"

"It's not spying on us or anything. It's just for listening."

42

"Yeah right. Just like our phones are just for phone calls and texts."

"Will you calm down?" Victoria spat. "You're so nervous about being caught that this isn't fun anymore. You're always looking over your shoulder —"

"And you're always looking for what's next!" Brooke glared at Victoria, and tried to ignore the blinking red lights of the beetle mocking her from beneath Victoria's hair. "You're obsessed with podcasts and how we can broadcast something that's supposed to be between us. And when you can't do that, you pipe in everyone else's murders while we're committing our own. Why do you need this?"

"Why do you need this to just be us? Think of what we could accomplish if we got online. Think of just how much we'd fuck this town over if we tapped into everyone who thinks they're doing an honest service for the good of the town. Think of the rush!"

Brooke folded her arms and glared at Victoria. "I already feel the rush," Brooke said. "Or at least, I did."

Victoria stood still, but even in the dark, Brooke could see she was stung. Brooke ignored it. "I'm not going to do this with you anymore," she said. "Not if you're going to wear that fucking thing when we do it, and not if you're going to spend all your time with those damn podcasts."

Victoria's hand swung to the beetle. Her fingers closed over it, as if to protect it. She quickly dropped her hand, but it was enough for Brooke to know where they stood. "No more," Brooke said as she stormed off. "Don't follow me."

"Brooke!"

"Call me when you can do this without a thousand digital voices telling you it's awesome." Brooke picked up her gait and sped out of the woods. She didn't want to see Victoria. She didn't want to see anyone or their damn beetles. She just wanted to go home.

————

Brooke didn't hear from Victoria. She tried not to feel hurt. She'd given Victoria a rule. Victoria followed it. Brooke just wished that it wasn't the one rule that kept them apart.

Brooke stayed low for the first few weeks. It grew difficult to ignore the chatter of others talking about those damn podcasts. More and more people in her life, from coworkers to family members to Lyft drivers, asked her if she was listening to the latest one. She always shook her head no.

When she didn't hear their chatter, she saw their beetles flickering in their ears. Bronze, then chrome, then silver; but all with blinking red eyes indicating that they were listening to someone's darkest secrets. Brooke hated the sight of them. She began to imagine slicing off their ears and stabbing the beetle repeatedly before dropping it into the river with its dead person.

Even in her imagination, though, her kills weren't the same without Victoria. Days became weeks. Brooke refused to be the first to call, and she imagined Victoria was doing the same.

One evening, after weeks had become months, Brooke took a walk through the park to clear her head. Someone darted past her and smacked into her elbow.

"Watch it!" she shouted. The runner didn't look back. Brooke heard footsteps and laughter behind her. She turned in time to see two more people run by.

They caught up with the man who'd bumped into her and descended on him like rats on a corpse.

"Stop!" the first runner yelled. "Please!"

"Take that, you filthy murderer," one of the attackers, a woman with a messy auburn bob, said as she brandished a large knife from her purse.

"I haven't killed anyone!"

"That's what they all say," the other attacker, a man with an Abercrombie haircut whose turtleneck peeked out from under his coat, said as he took out a hammer from his coat pocket.

The runner's cries became muffled, then gurgled, then silent. Brooke kept her distance, not wanting to fall victim to the madness of two killers. One person she could take by herself, but two …

The attackers laughed and propped up the runner's corpse. They took a selfie and held their free fingers in the shape of a V. "Score one for the Vigil!" the woman said. Brooke wondered if they were filming themselves. Either way, she turned to leave before she ended up caught on camera.

"We found him, Vickie!" the man said. "One of the killers, anyway."

Brooke halted. Vickie … it couldn't be. She sped home, the attackers' laughter fading behind her. She kept hearing the name over and over in her head. Vickie, Vickie, Vickie. The pounding wouldn't rest. In an attempt to quiet it, Brooke did a quick search for "Vickie" and "The Vigil." The top result was a podcast — of course it was a fucking podcast — called *Vickie's Vigilantes*. The podcast presented cold cases, leads, and clues for the average listener to track down suspects of the Hollingsworth Murders.

Brooke's blood turned as cold as the bodies she'd dumped in the pond over the past four years. Victoria was giving people clues about their murders. She was opening their jar of fireflies to Hollingsworth, and letting their glow lead everyone to her.

Brooke remembered the couple in the park. They'd run right past her, focused on the runner. The runner was a man, with a slight pudge and greying hair — nothing like her. If Victoria was giving Hollingsworth clues about the two of them, how could they have made such an obvious mistake?

Because, Brooke realized, they weren't mistaken. Victoria had led her listeners to a random man — one Victoria knew they would probably kill. She was leading people to innocents. It was the expanded empire she'd dreamed of in their final weeks of killing together.

The only way she'd know for sure would be to listen to an episode herself. Brooke clicked through to the podcast's website. She saw a message under New Episodes: "Due to the podcast's immense popularity, direct streaming isn't available. You can hear all episodes of *Vickie's Vigilantes* on your verified beetle device."

Brooke slammed her laptop closed. Those fucking beetles. She wouldn't put it past Victoria to have some kind of endorsement deal lined up for a little extra cash. Maybe she was leading the cops to her fans the way she led her fans to innocent people. Maybe she was leading everyone in Hollingsworth into a cat-and-mouse chase, with violent ends for both.

But Brooke couldn't know for sure — not when she wasn't listening to Victoria's podcast.

———

Brooke grew used to the beetle in her ear. Its metal was warm, and she mostly kept it in sleep mode until there was a new episode of *Vickie's Vigilantes* to listen to. She didn't bother trying to find the people Victoria led her listeners to — she could find victims all on her own if she wanted to. Rather, she listened for clues in the background to try and find Victoria's whereabouts. A rustle of trees, heavy traffic, an errant cat — something that would help her find her friend. She couldn't deny that every time Victoria's voice seeped through the beetle, she felt a warm bit of comfort.

In her latest episode, Victoria promised a special surprise for anyone who could solve her latest puzzle. "Find the pond where no one plays," she said. "Where all you'll see are fireflies."

Brooke had perked up at "fireflies." She wondered if Victoria was calling her. She wondered if Victoria knew she was listening.

There was only one way to find out.

She walked through Briar Park and took the short cut to the pond where they'd caught fireflies as children. Where they'd first met all those years ago, where they'd played with other kids and soon abandoned them for each other. Brooke's heartbeat rose with every step closer to the clearing. She passed through the bushes, and saw the pond in front of her.

No one else was there. Brooke stood still, and looked at the water. She felt the choked sting of a lump in her throat. Victoria hadn't been calling her. Victoria didn't want to see her anymore.

"There she is!"

Brooke looked to her left, and saw the woman she'd first seen kill the stranger in the park move towards her with an ugly smile. The same man as before followed behind. "So you're the reason everyone's disappeared, huh?" the woman asked.

Brooke wasn't the only reason they'd disappeared — but only Brooke would die that night. She took a step back, but didn't speak. She knew how fast this couple was. She should've known she would be led into a trap. She deserved whatever came next.

"Not even gonna run, huh?" the man said with a sneer. He pulled a hammer from his coat. "Smart."

He lifted the hammer, then froze. The woman paused as she unsheathed her knife. "Cole?" she said.

Cole sputtered around a burst of blood that oozed from his mouth. A knife appeared from behind him and sliced open his neck. He fell to the ground. Victoria stood behind him.

"Cole!" the woman screamed. She glared at Victoria. "What the fuck? He's not a killer!"

"Isn't he?" Victoria said in a high-pitched voice, one that sounded nothing like her podcast voice or even her regular speaking voice. "The Vigil said he was by the pond."

Brooke's eyes widened, but she set herself straight before the woman could see her. "We're part of the Vigil," the woman said. She sped towards Victoria and took out her knife. "I can't believe you killed him, you fucking —"

She stopped her stride as Brooke plunged her knife into her back. Brooke stabbed her once, twice — ten times. The rush intensified with every plunge.

Once the woman lay limp, Brooke sliced off her ear and hacked her beetle into pieces.

"You really hate those things, don't you?" Victoria said.

Brooke looked up, and saw Victoria wearing a small smirk. Brooke smiled a little and brushed back the hair over her left ear. "I really do. They never shut up."

"Tap the back legs — left one, then right one — four times."

48

Brooke did so. The beetle not only quieted, but fell limp from her ear. Brooke caught it before it shattered on the ground.

"Despite what you think —" Victoria brushed back her hair and revealed a bare ear — "I don't always need one in my ear."

"Why?"

"They get annoying sometimes. I run a podcast, I don't need to listen to them all the time —"

"I mean, why this clue? Did you know I was coming?"

"I hoped you would. I put this together because I missed killing people myself. I was going to surprise the first people from the Vigil, kill a couple of them, then set my listeners on another hunt. It gets old just hearing about other people having all the fun. But —" Victoria gave Brooke a sheepish smile. "But I also gave a clue I figured you'd follow on the off-chance you were listening. I hoped you'd come because it wouldn't be the same without you. Killing, celebrating … whispering. I'd give up a thousand voices in my ear to hear yours."

Brooke opened her hand and held up the deactivated beetle. "And I'd give up silence to hear yours in mine."

Victoria smiled. Brooke thought she saw the glimmer of tears in her eyes. She was about to tease her, when a voice from the other side of the pond called, "There you are!"

Brooke and Victoria turned, and saw a young man with a hockey stick moving towards them. Brooke knew they could take him. She felt a rush she hadn't felt since graduation begin to flutter in her brain like wings.

Victoria grinned as she lifted up her blade. "Let's get one more fan before we go."

"Sounds good," Brooke said. "But I get the ear."

49

# AS QUICK AS POISON

In the darkness, liquid pooled
Upon a table in the wood.

A bottle lay inside her hand,
Its poison seeping through the land.

She'd thought a drink would calm her nerves,
That one last sip would stop the stirs

Of voices crawling in her mind
Which fed her thoughts and dreams unkind.

But when she drank that fatal cup
And took a moment to look up,

She fell to earth. Her time had passed
As quick as poison through a glass.

# CRANBERRY

*Content warning: eating disorders and body dysmorphia*

Christy's favorite holiday was Thanksgiving. She loved the fancy tablecloth her mother set out, and loved watching her father carve the turkey. Christy wasn't allowed to help — at eight years old, she was still too young to handle a knife — but her father let her watch so she would know how to do it when she was older. He slipped her a piece of skin, and she loved the way it cracked in her mouth and coated her tongue with salt and grease.

She ate her piece of turkey skin with a smile as her mother opened a can of cranberry sauce and poured it in a bowl. The sauce came out as a cylinder and kept its form, with the ridges of the can rippling down the sides.

Christy and her parents laughed at the sight of it. "It kind of looks like you," her father said as he pinched a roll of fat on Christy's waist.

Christy lost her smile. Her mother chuckled softly as she cut the cranberry sauce with a butter knife. It fell to pieces in the bowl, which her mother topped with walnuts.

"Going to enjoy that sauce, Cranberry?" her dad said, smiling and pinching her fat one more time. He returned to carving the turkey. Christy swallowed the skin and felt it scratch her throat on the way down.

Christy had always known she was more plump than normal. The kids at school called her fat before whatever insult they wanted to throw her way. Fat nerd. Fat idiot. Fat girl. Fat was what they saw first. Christy had learned to absorb their insults and turn them into white noise.

It was harder, though, to ignore her parents. Christy noticed as they watched her plate and took note of how much food disappeared, and how quickly. She could almost hear them counting the pounds she added to her waist, pounds that formed rings which showed her to the world the way the rings of a trunk showed the age of a tree.

As Christy grew, she tried to stop her rings from growing with her. Her breasts grew out, but so did her stomach. The hair on her belly and legs was only made worse by the fat it covered. The monthly bleeding made her feel less bloated, but not less fat. She tried to eat well, tried to eat her fruits and vegetables and keep the candy down to treats at Halloween and Christmas. It was never enough.

On the day before the start of ninth grade, and after a back-to-school shopping session where her mother had clucked about shopping for larger sizes, Christy stood naked and alone in her room. She pushed the fat until her skin was against her bones. She sighed as she looked at her newfound waist, set in perfect symmetry with her hips and her breasts. She pulled the fat beneath her chin and tucked it under her thumbs. Her jawbone peeked at her, her skin stretched against her skull. She kneaded her arms and legs, the bones pressing against her muscles and showing her what they could offer. Approval. Appeal. Affection. She wished her bones would slice through the fat and take their rightful place against her skin.

Wishing, though, wasn't enough. Christy had to make it happen herself — and she had to try harder than she'd ever tried before.

Christy took extra care as high school progressed and her body grew into itself. She imagined her parents watching her every bite even when she was at school. She chose the healthiest foods, took longer walks, tried to do crunches in her room. Nothing worked — until, suddenly, it did.

All of a sudden, Christy's efforts clicked into place. Her diet smoothies, scant peanut-butter sandwiches, and long walks began to pay off. Her clothes got bigger and she grew smaller. She lost weight — noticeable weight — and it stayed off. She graduated from high school with the body she'd longed for ever since she was a little girl and first felt her folds spill over her jeans.

"Have fun," her mother said as they finished moving Christy into her college dorm.

"Watch out for the dining hall," her father joked as he patted her waist.

Her mother chuckled. "The freshman fifteen is always a killer." She winked at Christy.

Christy waited until they were gone before she allowed her smile to disappear. She ran her hands over her waist, her chest, her chin and her shoulders. She felt the bones beneath, and felt comforted by how they pressed against her skin. As long as she could feel the bones, she'd be okay.

Christy made sure throughout her first semester that the feel of her bones never left her palms. She monitored her plate at the dining hall. She was extra careful with dessert. If she allowed herself an indulgence, like a cookie or a brownie, she thought of her former self with every bite to remind herself to not gain weight and lose her bones. Dessert became so stressful that she almost avoided it altogether. Eating was a game of chance — one that Christy was determined not to lose.

Christy avoided gaining weight, and did one better by losing more. She felt her tapered waist and the ceiling of her ribs. She'd lie down and feel her hip bones jut out over her waistband. As long as she could feel her bones, she knew she was safe.

Christy came home for Thanksgiving feeling proud. She didn't even mind the sight of the rippled mold of cranberry sauce falling into the bowl, its rolls of jellied fat quivering into place. Her father chuckled as her mother grabbed a butter knife.

"The sauce has its ribs sticking out," he said as he pinched Christy's bones. "Kind of like you, Cranberry."

The nickname struck Christy in the heart. She could feel her heart ramming against her ribs. The ribs and bones that added to her body, that stuck out, that made it so large that it was always in the way.

The scraping of metal against ceramic rang in Christy's ears. Christy watched her mother slice the cranberry sauce into manageable pieces, watched her father carve the turkey and set the salted skin in pieces on the plate. That was the only way she could be perfect. It was the only way that any of them could be perfect.

Her mind, her heart, and her bones clanged and scraped inside of her so loudly she could barely hear her father shout when she wrested the knife from his grasp. She could hardly feel her mother's hands pull at her wrist as she took the blade to her waist.

They all would be in pieces soon. Soon, they all would be perfect.

# DROPS

Milla loved the sound of summer storms. She closed her eyes as rain rushed down the window. She'd spent all afternoon tiptoeing through the house so as not to disturb her mother, and a pause to take in the sound of rain was the perfect way to satisfy her own desire for solitude.

The rain began to dissipate, and soon, she heard only the patter of drops. She opened her eyes as the sun began to warm her. Milla hoped she'd see a rainbow.

When she opened her eyes, she saw sunshine, but no rain. Still, she heard drops — and she heard them to her left.

Milla turned and saw her younger sister Reece. Milla frowned. "What are you doing up so early from your nap?" she asked. "You don't want to —"

Before she could warn Reece not to wake their mother, Milla saw a trail of urine trickle onto the hardwood floor. It flowed from Reece's legs in a stream towards the carpet. Reece stared behind Milla as if she weren't there.

"Reece!" Milla jumped up from her chair. "Why don't you go to the bathroom?"

"Because Toby's in there," said her mother's voice from behind her.

Milla turned and faced her mother. Her mother smiled, a crescent moon that shone above the river of blood on her neck and chest. Drops fell from her knife onto the floor.

"I'm sorry," she said as she walked towards Milla and Reece. "The rain woke me up."

# SNOWFALL

Lila gasped when she looked out her window. A blanket of snow covered the field that lay beyond her house. It stretched as far as the blackened trees that made up the surrounding woods.

Before her mother could wake and ask her to do her morning chores, Lila pulled on her snow boots and winter coat. She ran outside and was struck immediately by stillness. Everything around her was quiet. She heard no birds, no wind, no rustling grass. The stillness was peaceful. She wanted to absorb it all.

The woods stood covered in snow. Normally Lila avoided the forest. Her mother told her not to play there at night, and that warning usually kept her out during the day as well. But something about this day, and the peaceful snow on the empty branches, beckoned Lila to take part in nature's serenity. She walked past her yard and into the woods, the footprints in the snow the only disturbance she left behind.

The sky, already gray with cloud cover, took on the color of steel when blotted out by the trees. Lila looked around her, ever watchful for a wolf or a strange man, or the other monsters her mother had warned her were within the woods. All Lila saw, though, were trees. All she heard was silence.

She breathed in and took in the cold. The chill pierced her lungs and stung her nostrils, but the pain gave a slight sense of pleasure. She noticed a snowbank unbroken by paw prints. She felt an urge to lie in it, perhaps to make a snow angel and leave her mark in this winter sanctuary.

She lay down and felt the coldness wrap its arms around her. She heard her own breathing as she laid her head in the snow. In, then out, in, then out — like waves on the beach or snow in the wind.

Lila closed her eyes and held her breath. She heard an exhale beneath her, a staggered purr that wasn't her own.

Lila opened her eyes and saw the snow surrounding her body. It seemed to grow beside her. She realized she was sinking, the dirt below giving way to her body like a pool of water.

A tree root meandered over her body, as if trapping her in its sleep. She gasped and felt a rush of cold stab her throat and her lungs.

Her scream froze before it escaped her lips.

All she heard as she sank below the snow was the gentle sound of breathing: in, then out. In, then out.

# DEATH IS A HUNTER

Maddie sighed as she walked through a field. "How long until we get there?" she asked.

"Soon," Dylan replied.

Maddie pouted. She'd lived next door to Dylan her whole life, and until today, he'd never wanted to play with her. He never showed interest, probably because he was a boy and because he was five years older than her.

But Dylan came to her today, and asked if she wanted to play in the woods. Maddie loved the woods. She played there almost every day. Dylan had insisted they cut through the field, and because he was fifteen — almost a grownup — Maddie had listened.

After a long time walking, though, she began to regret it. "Why doesn't the field have a path?" she asked. She thought of the paths in the woods that were littered with paw prints from Mousie, the gray stray tabby cat her mother said she shouldn't touch. "I wish we could make one."

"We'd need a scythe," Dylan said.

"What's a scythe?"

"A long blade. Reapers hold them."

"Reapers?"

"Ghosts that gather souls."

Maddie smiled at the spooky image. As they approached the woods, she remembered a TV show her mother had watched about men who lived in the woods and carved animal skins with long, thick blades. "If they have blades, then wouldn't they be hunters?" she asked.

"Maybe."

"I bet Death is a hunter." Maddie had seen Mousie pouncing on birds, and snakes snatching up mice. "I bet reapers have eyes like cats, and chase souls until they fill their bellies —"

"Maddie, be quiet. You don't want to attract animals."

"None of the animals will bother me. Not even the mountain lions."

"Hush."

Maddie clamped her mouth shut. They walked in silence, the sun moving from the top of the sky towards the tops of the trees with each minute past, until at last, they reached the woods. They moved down a path she hadn't walked before. It opened into a dark clearing with a small pond.

Maddie gasped and rushed forward. "A secret pond! How did you find it?"

"It's mine," said a deep voice to her right. Maddie turned and saw an older man, much older than Dylan, with blood-stained overalls. She turned to call for Dylan, but she saw him walk back into the trees. Calling for him wouldn't help.

"It's my special pond," the man continued. "Where I hide special girls like you."

Maddie closed her eyes and prayed that the forest would help her. The man moved closer. She could smell rot on his breath.

A hiss sounded through the clearing. Maddie opened her eyes and saw a flash of gray streak towards the man. Mousie leapt onto his neck and dug her claws in tight. The man screamed as blood streamed from his skin over her paws. He tore Mousie from his neck, but before he could throw her, he screamed again and dropped her. A cluster of snakes slithered up his legs, their fangs in view and looking for a place to bite. The man fell to the ground as the snakes moved up his body. They each took turns biting into his skin.

The snakes scattered. But the man wasn't safe. A mountain lion jumped into the clearing, blood and drool dripping from her maw. She looked up at Maddie, her eyes green and glistening. She almost seemed to thank her for the prey. Then she grabbed the man by the neck and dragged him into the forest.

Mousie rubbed against Maddie's legs and purred. Maddie smiled as she stroked Mousie's fur.

# QUADRAPOCALYPSE

The train lurched as the Metro moved towards Foggy Bottom. It was moving through the tunnel Morgan always wished they'd leave the fastest, the one connecting Virginia to DC, beneath the Potomac River. She tried to avoid thinking about how she spent a portion of each day underwater just to get to work. Those thoughts inevitably led to wondering about just how strong the tunnel walls were against the river's current.

Like her fellow commuters, though, she managed to distract herself from such thoughts and make it into the District each day. Some people read the paper, others listened to music. Morgan read a book. Her commute was the best time to read.

Lurch. "Train moving," the conductor said.

Stop. "Train holding. We thank you for your patience."

She'd heard that refrain at least four times. Morgan sighed as she put away her book. She couldn't read with the train pitching her body back and forth.

Morgan's eyes wandered across her fellow passengers. Most of them stared into nothingness as they waited to get to work. One passenger, a woman in a yolk-yellow raincoat, looked into nothingness for a long time. She seemed lost in thought, so lost in thought that she was the only one who didn't notice when she dropped her phone.

It landed with a thud that snapped the commuters from their distractions. A chorus of variations on "Ma'am, you dropped your phone" and "Is it broken?" rang through the train. The woman waved in thanks as she picked it up. The screen had cracked, and Morgan saw its jagged smile, a kaleidoscope of broken light and pixels on its shattered face. Morgan thought she saw four shadows fly past people's feet. She blinked, as did the lights on the train.

The lights came back on. Morgan shook her head, and figured the shadows were just from the lights.

Morgan noticed that the train was still holding. It hadn't moved an inch.

"We'll be holding here momentarily. Thank you for your patience."

The commuters sighed and rolled their eyes. A group of tourists stared at the Metro map as they hoped to find their way around the city. Morgan studied the map to give herself something to do, even though she knew the city well already. The map was a colorful spider whose legs wrapped around the District's four corners: Northwest, Northeast, Southeast, and Southwest. The Metro's lines extended to all of the city's quadrants. Morgan wondered where everyone would go once they were released.

--------

**Southeast**

Danica cursed as she skidded across the slick granite sidewalk in her heels. She walked as fast as she could through the drizzle. She had a lunch meeting at Tortilla Coast, and she was already late. The damp sidewalks didn't help, but the slow-moving congressional aides and tourists visiting Capitol Hill were what really slowed her down.

*Why are there still so many people out in this rain?* she thought with a frown as she maneuvered around fellow pedestrians and tried not to poke them with her umbrella. It'd been raining off and on almost all week. At least today, it was just a persistent drizzle and not a downpour.

Danica heard a gurgling sound below her. She looked down, then saw burst of water spit up through the manhole ahead of her and onto the road.

A group of staffers cursed as the cuffs of their pants were dampened. Danica shook her head. Even though today's rain was just a drizzle, one had to expect residual flooding from the Potomac to find its way onto the city's streets.

More water spewed from the manhole. Danica saw that manholes down the sidewalk did the same. She looked back at the one closest to her, transfixed, along with several others.

The next sputter brought a wave of putrid water and what looked like paws and feet within its current. Danica covered her mouth as the water trickled away and the paws, feet, and fur hobbled into a standing position.

"A rat!" a man next to her cried. Several rats peered at their newfound place above ground. They were so laden with water that their bellies protruded and rippled as they moved along the street. Despite their weight, they moved quickly towards the people staring at them.

A blonde woman acted quickly — she stabbed a rat with her umbrella before it could crawl over her shoes. It popped like a balloon, water mixed with blood and guts flying onto her dress.

She held up her umbrella in triumph, but the victory was short-lived. The water didn't run off of her legs, but rather up her body. She seemed to dissolve under its current. Her clothes blackened into mildew and her screams became garbled as mud spewed from her throat.

The others weren't much better off. The rats crawled over their bodies, their fur leaving slicked trails across their skin that turned people's bodies to algae and mold. They became green and oily remnants of flesh, ones that washed away beneath the drizzle.

Danica turned and ran before the rats could reach her. The sidewalk beneath her grew softer with every step. The rats and water spewing from the manholes seemed to be turning the sidewalk into a muddied shore, one that would soon be as thick and damp as an ocean floor.

Danica's sprint ended as the heel of her shoe dug into the sidewalk. She twisted it off and ran further, hoping that the increasing slickness on her foot was only from the rain on the sidewalk.

––––––––––

**Southwest**

Andre tied his apron as he prepared to open the crab shack. He was alone, as he was every morning. He liked to arrive before anyone else so that his food would be ready all the quicker. His fellow restaurant owners were his neighbors and friends, but they were also his competition.

He'd worked on the wharf for almost twenty years, long before the wharf officially became "the Wharf," with strings of lights along the dock that led potential customers to concert halls, distilleries, and expensive restaurants.

Still, people came to his shack each day wanting a steaming plate of crabs covered in Old Bay to eat by the water. Andre just hoped they could reach him. The rain all week had flooded the docks, and only a raised wooden bridge allowed hungry customers passage.

A loud pop distracted Andre from preparing his pans. He looked toward the new restaurants on the Wharf. One of the lights on the string along the dock had exploded. It set off an identical pop. Each bulb burst, one by one. Sparks flew up as the shards of glass flew out.

Andre moved to the counter so he could see. The sparks weren't small by any means. They looked like orange snakes that spiraled and coiled around the buildings. As they wrapped around the structures, each burst into flames. They crackled and hissed as the dock connecting them became a river of flame flowing into the water.

Andre pulled out his cellphone, ready to call the fire department. Before he could, the sound of an explosion burst to his left. The streetlamps began to explode. Snakes and sparks did not come forth. These creatures of fire were much bigger. They flew from the glass, wings of red and blue crackling against the sky as they soared further east. They ran their hands along the sidewalk and grass like people letting their fingers loll in the water during a boat ride. Everything they touched turned to fire. It was a flame without smoke, and burned without turning things to ash.

Andre looked at the wooden platform leading to his crab shack, then the water surrounding it on all sides. He'd never been so grateful for a flood before.

A flicker of light caught his attention. He looked beyond the platform. The pyre that had been the Wharf did not extinguish when it touched the water. It continued to burn, using the river as oil for its flame.

Andre looked back down. He saw tiny snakes of gold swimming through the flooded waters toward his restaurant, like minnows rushing towards a morning snack.

---

**Northeast**

Portia just wanted to get to class, but the bustle of H Street made that nearly impossible. She'd been promised that the budding H Street Corridor would be the perfect place for a college student to study and party in the District. The marketing downplayed how long it would take to get from H Street to Howard University, and how often she'd be waiting for a bus if she wanted to party anywhere but H Street's overpriced clubs and hipster restaurants.

She walked with a frown as she adjusted her backpack. A truck drove by and belched a cloud of smoke. Portia waved the smoke from her face and tried not to breathe it in, though she could feel it settle in her nostrils. She made a mental note to use her neti pot that night.

A breeze blew the smoke away faster than her hand could hope to accomplish. Portia smiled and thanked God for a bit of wind to help her on her commute.

"Ow!"

Portia looked towards the cry, and saw a man on the sidewalk in front of her. He stood up and brushed gravel from his knees. He saw Portia looking at him. Before she could turn away, he smiled and shrugged. "Guess the wind caught me off-guard," he said with a laugh.

Portia gave a small smile back. He was cute — even though he sported an unfortunate man bun — and had a nice laugh.

Both were distracted from the other by two more screams to their left. They turned and saw a family of three sprawled on the sidewalk. The child, who looked no older than five, began to cry. His parents lay stunned on the ground.

"Are you okay?" Portia called as she rushed towards them. A gust of wind stopped her. It froze her in her tracks, then knocked her to the ground. "Ow!" she screamed as she rubbed her aching butt.

"Let me help —" the cute man began to say, but he was pushed back down before he could make it to her. He seemed to be pulled back by an invisible hook. Portia skidded across the sidewalk. Though the wind whipped through her clothes, she swore she felt a multitude of fingers grip her body and pull her back.

People all around her skidded and fell on the sidewalk, as if they were being bandied about by small, invisible hands. Portia didn't know what to make of the wind. It was drizzly today, but not stormy; and hurricane season was still weeks away.

The wind grew stronger. More people fell, and with greater force. Heads began to crack and bleed on the sidewalk. Skinned knees turned into scraped bodies. Portia watched in horror as the cute man was lifted by a gust of wind and thrown through the glass of the Irish pub she'd just had dinner in the night before.

She screamed as she was lifted off the ground, then dropped with a thud on the curb. Another truck rolled by, and she thanked God that she'd fallen on the curb and not on the street. She grabbed onto a streetlamp to try and stay steady.

The truck came to a stop, held back and knocked about by the wind. Before it fell, it belched out one last cloud of smoke.

Portia didn't register the truck blowing over, nor the screams of the people crushed beneath it. All she saw was the large, outstretched hand that the truck's exhaust made visible. Just before the wind blew the smoke into nothing, she saw clawed fingers stretch and zoom towards her, ready to bat her away.

———————

**Northwest**

Gita's favorite thing about her apartment was the view of the zoo. It was surrounded by lush trees and shoots of bamboo. She could see the tops of the trees from her top-floor apartment, and she liked to imagine all of the animals living there beneath the canopy.

She stirred milk into her morning tea and checked her phone while she sipped. An alert from the *Woodley Park Buzz*, their neighborhood e-newsletter, blinked up at her:

*Zookeepers ask neighborhood to be on alert for a missing flamingo from the zoo. Do not approach. Email bird's location to —*

Gita didn't read the rest. She remembered when a red panda had gone missing for almost two days. Someone found it in their backyard. Someone would likely find the flamingo resting in their koi pond, or dipping its beak into one of the puddles left over from the flash flooding in Rock Creek Park.

Gita set down her tea and looked back outside. The rain had left the trees and bamboo looking even more lush than before. They almost seemed to be sitting outside of her balcony.

Another alert beeped from her phone. Gita read another note from the *Woodley Park Buzz*:

*Zookeepers ask neighborhood to be on alert for a missing orangutan from the zoo. Do not approach. Email orangutan's —*

Gita furrowed her brow as she set down her phone. An orangutan had never escaped from the zoo before. She figured, though, that an orangutan would be easy to spot once Woodley Park was on the lookout for it. There were trees, but not many. People would notice an orangutan on the loose.

She looked back outside. Her eyes widened. The view looked more like a forest than it had before. The trees blotted out the sky and seemed to surround her building on all sides. It had to be an illusion, her eyes playing tricks on her as she took in all the green that had come from the week's rain.

Horns began to blare from the street below. Gita rolled her eyes, then walked towards the living room window, which looked out over the street. It was her least favorite view, as it reminded her that she was very much in a city. Normally she'd ignore it, but a part of her wondered if the orangutan was in the street.

Gita looked out and almost dropped her phone. Vines as thick as rope shot into the street from all sides. They carved through buildings and cracked the pavement. A menagerie of zoo animals ran over their newfound bridge to freedom.

The human residents of Woodley Park weren't so lucky. Cars and people were coiled in the foliage and slammed against buildings. One shop owner tried to take a knife to a vine coming for his window. The vine wrapped around his leg, and two leaves grabbed his knife. Gita looked away just as the leaf placed the blade against the shop owner's throat.

Gita's phone beeped once more. She looked down and read yet another note from the *Woodley Park Buzz*:

*Zookeepers ask neighborhood to be on alert for a missing tiger from the zoo. Do not —*

A loud crash interrupted her. Gita turned, wondering with mounting fear if she'd see the tiger standing in her kitchen. Like the animals that climbed from the zoo to the street, it could have used the trees and bamboo outside her window as a ladder.

The trees and bamboo she loved to look out over each morning crashed through her table and spilled her tea. The branches and vines moved towards her as quickly as centipedes moving through dirt. They wrapped around her ankles, and Gita cried out as their flesh stung her skin. The vines yanked her onto the floor and dragged her towards her overgrown balcony. Her phone beeped one last time as it flew from her hands.

————

**Metro**

"We're continuing to hold. Thank you for your patience."

Morgan had lost track of how long they'd been holding. She'd already finished her book, and had grown tired of looking at the same frustrated passengers over and over again. No one could get any signal in the tunnel. No one knew when they would be moving — not even the train conductor, who simply assured them they'd be moving momentarily.

A loud crash broke everyone from their frustrated trance. Morgan looked out the window, but didn't see anything.

The crash sounded again. The car in front of them knocked against the tunnel's walls, as if punched by the wind. Morgan wondered how wind could get underground.

The crash was replaced by a pop. A blaze of fire shot past the train. It almost appeared to have wings. There was a thud on top of the car. The ceiling dissolved like ice cream on a sidewalk, and flaming claws seeped through the metal.

As frightened passengers fled, a vine crashed through the emergency exit. It coiled around the metal poles and broke through the seats. Passengers tried to move to the next car, but the wind that knocked the car in front of them punched passengers into the waiting hands of the flames and the plants.

Morgan hid under her seat and looked for an opening. She thought she saw the woman in the yolk-yellow raincoat slip away with a smile as a family of tourists ran from the vines. She looked at the walls of the tunnel, and wished that the river she feared so much would wash away the fire and foliage.

Morgan heard water, but not from the walls.

A putrid stream trickled into the train, dissolving the carpet and turning the seats into mildew. She watched as the elements did away with them all.

Morgan heard one last call over everyone's screams: "We'll be holding here momentarily. Thank you for your patience."

# HOLLOW

Mrs. Sassafras was Lindsay's favorite doll. Lindsay had spotted Mrs. Sassafras at the church rummage sale, her porcelain cheeks dull and her linen dress yellowed. But it was her eyes that drew Lindsay in. Their irises were gone, perhaps faded with time.

Wherever they'd gone, Lindsay didn't care. She wanted the doll, and once her mother bought Mrs. Sassafras, she became her favorite.

Lindsay liked that Mrs. Sassafras couldn't look at her. Her mother often looked at her with a sigh; her teachers with frustration as she answered questions wrong; her classmates with mocking laughter as they asked why she was so quiet. Her cousin Bethany, who was her age and also in her class, was the worst. She always picked on her, both at home and at school. She pretended she wasn't Lindsay's cousin when she was around her friends, but being related gave Bethany so much more to tease her about.

The teasing and laughter were too much to bear, but Mrs. Sassafras made it better. Lindsay would hug her close when things got bad, when her usual sadness instead became an overwhelming darkness that clouded her mind. Mrs. Sassafras didn't care if Lindsay emanated darkness. Mrs. Sassafras couldn't see her.

Bethany saw her every Sunday, when Aunt Noelle and Uncle Howard would come over for dinner. Bethany was always sent upstairs to play with Lindsay, and she spent that time taking Lindsay's toys, bragging about how many more friends she had or how her grades were better, or making fun of Lindsay's outfit.

One Sunday, Bethany's teasing expanded to Mrs. Sassafras. "What an ugly doll," Bethany said with a sneer as she picked her up.

"Put her down," Lindsay said as she sped towards Bethany. She wouldn't let Bethany ruin Mrs. Sassafras.

"Of course you'd love a doll as ugly as you are."

"Give her to me!"

Bethany threw Mrs. Sassafras on the ground.

The doll's face cracked and her arm broke off. The arm lay on the floor, its end in jagged shards.

Lindsay dropped to her knees and picked up the arm, blinking back tears.

"You're crying over a doll?" Bethany laughed. It was the ugliest sound Lindsay had ever heard. She wanted it to end. She knew how to end it.

Lindsay stood up and smacked Bethany across the face with Mrs. Sassafras' arm.

Bethany fell down, her eyes wide in both shock and pain. Lindsay was ignited by Bethany's fear. She struck Bethany again, then again.

Bethany's cheek began to bleed, and her cries grew less with every blow.

Lindsay dealt one final, deep blow to Bethany's head. Blood trickled from the cuts on Bethany's face, and she lay still.

Lindsay dropped the arm and picked up Mrs. Sassafras. Blood smattered her cracked porcelain cheeks, and she stared at Lindsay with hollow eyes. She smiled at their emptiness.

She closed her eyes and brought Mrs. Sassafras' cheek to hers, whispering, "I love you."

# STICK FIGURE FAMILY

Chelsea hurried through the parking lot at Trader Joe's. It was always crazy on Saturdays, and she usually tried to avoid the hubbub of suburban parents and their cranky kids. She'd run out of her favorite soap that morning, though, and would need more before the weekend was over.

The parking lot was a quagmire of vans, shopping carts, and people. A couple bickered over something trivial as they walked by her. A child screamed in her cart as her father tried to sweet-talk her into behaving.

Chelsea closed her eyes as she tried to keep her composure.

"Watch out!" a woman's voice called.

Chelsea looked toward the voice, then felt sharp plastic whack against her legs. She cursed, and a woman in a blue knitted poncho pulled back the cart that had hit her.

"I'm sorry," the woman said. "I was lost in my own world and didn't even see you."

Chelsea glared at her and rubbed her aching knees.

The woman had straight brown hair, as dull and faded as her grey leggings. She pressed a button and unlocked the minivan next to them. Chelsea saw a line of stick figures on the window. She tried not to roll her eyes. Stick figure families were so sickeningly charming. *No one cares how many smiling kids you have*, she thought.

"Do you need something?" the woman asked. She had the slightest hint of irritation in her voice. She had some nerve, being the one who hit Chelsea in the first place.

"No," Chelsea said. She walked off without a word. All she needed was to get out of the parking lot.

———

Camila checked her hair in the mirror before pulling out of the parking lot at Trader Joe's. She hadn't even seen that girl with the messy blonde bun and the deep-set frown. She wondered what was wrong with her. Hitting her with the cart had been an accident — an honest mistake. Camila sighed as she pulled out of the lot and turned on the radio. The girl wasn't her concern.

She drove down the road. The strip malls and condos disappeared behind her as she made her way towards her favorite spot: the lake behind her parents' old cabin. It was her favorite spot to be alone and catch her breath after a busy morning chasing after the kids.

Camila parked her van and took in the sparkling lake in front of her. The surface lay still, with no one around to drop rocks in its waters or cast lines in search of fish.

She smiled as she opened the trunk. She had a box of crackers and a block of her favorite cheese waiting for her.

Camila set the grocery bag on the ground, then lifted the limp bodies of two children from the floor of the trunk. They'd been running through the woods near her apartment, and they should've known better than to wake her up with their shouts.

Once they were in the lake — and once she'd washed her hands — Camila ate her snack and stared out over the water. The surface bubbled a little as the bodies sank, but it soon stood as still as it had before.

Camila got to her feet and brushed stray blades of grass from her leggings. She approached her van, then dug through her purse. Before she got in, she stuck two new stick figures on her van's back window.

# HEARTS ARE JUST "LIKES"

Hailey's fingers trembled as she steadied her phone. It was always difficult to get her best side just right, but when she did, the result was beautiful. Her dimple appeared, her freckles sparkled, and her hair fell in a way that accented her eyes.

Of course, there were filters and Photoshop, but Hailey liked to keep her selfies as real as possible. Being real was what made her so popular online. Being real was what got her a like from Kim Kardashian when Hailey posted a photo of herself spritzing on Kim's new perfume and tagged her. Being real made thousands of strangers flock to her account to fill her feed with likes, and led hundreds of companies to offer her samples of their own perfumes, or their foods, or their lotions, or whatever Hailey could promote on their behalf by being a real face for their real product.

Hailey had a job to do on Instagram, a job that brought in likes and money. She'd do anything to keep it. Fortunately, all she had to do was take her picture.

Before snapping her latest selfie, Hailey angled the camera a little more to the left. She didn't want the splash of blood on the wall to be visible. She smiled, then took her picture. It had 3,000 likes within two minutes.

————

Hailey had many admirers who posted compliments, both kind and lewd, on her feed. TommyBoy89 was one she'd noticed amidst the din of all the rest. TommyBoy89 showered her with hearts, and liked every single one of her posts. It wasn't long before she noticed his photo next to his likes. She clicked through to his profile and saw a pair of beautiful eyes looking into hers, and a smile that was just as lovely.

Hailey liked his latest picture, and added a comment: *You like so many of my pics. Why don't you say hi?*

TommyBoy89 didn't respond. Hailey shrugged and forgot about her comment until the next day, when she posted a selfie with a tamarind bubble tea from a new café in Georgetown — complimentary, of course, so long as she tagged the café and added #yum in addition to #ad.

TommyBoy89 liked her photo within three minutes — and shortly after, he added a comment: *Hi.*

Hailey followed him and immediately sent a direct message so they could talk in private. They introduced themselves and found out the basics: they both lived in DC, they both spent a lot of time on social media, they were the same age and liked the same restaurants. It didn't take long to meet at an Italian place they both liked, and because the small talk was out of the way, it didn't take long for Hailey to invite TommyBoy89 — who had asked her to call him Tom — to her apartment, where they spent the rest of the night and the better part of the morning having sex.

They became a couple and began to post online together. Tom had a bit of a following himself — not quite as large as Hailey's, but large enough to where they could be considered an Instagram power couple. Hailey's selfies were interspersed with pictures of Tom looking over her shoulder, and her comments were frequently littered with starry-eyed followers declaring the two of them to be #relationshipgoals.

Hailey wondered if they'd feel the same if they noticed that Tom's likes had disappeared in time with them becoming close. After they'd been together for almost six months, her likes — and subsequent offers from companies to promote their products and enhance her brand — continued to skyrocket. However, none of those likes had come from TommyBoy89.

"Why aren't you liking my pictures anymore?" Hailey asked one day as they sat sprawled on her couch.

"I'm in a bunch of them," Tom answered as he scrolled through Instagram. "I feel weird liking my own face."

"There are plenty without you."

"I can tell you I like them in person." He leaned forward and kissed her cheek. "I like how your hair looks today, and those coconut pancakes you made this morning were delicious."

Hailey smiled, but didn't laugh. "I miss your hearts though," she said with a pout that was only somewhat fake.

"Hearts are just likes." Tom kissed her temple. "And I don't just like you. I love you."

"I love you, too." But her answer was distant, her thoughts lost in her feed as she scrolled through and saw he'd been liking everyone's photos but hers. It was hard to ignore the way his hearts were speckled across other accounts, boosting their presence and lessening hers. Hearts were important. Hearts kept her in business. Hearts weren't just likes — they were what kept her alive.

Tom insisted, though, that they weren't a big deal. Their disagreement on the matter began to cool things between them, though they were all smiles when they posted pictures online. Hailey wondered if he stayed with her to keep his gained popularity online, attaching himself to her influence. If that were the case, the least he could do was keep her afloat by liking just one of her damn posts.

"Jesus Christ, Hailey, will you lay off of me?" It was their third fight in two weeks. Hailey had posted several photos ahead of her weekly Instagram Live, and Tom hadn't liked a single one, not even the one where Hailey wrote *I love you, Tom* while making a heart with her fingers. "It's not that important!" he said.

"It is!" Hailey cried. "It's a video I want people to see, where we'll tell everyone we're moving in together for our six-month anniversary! How's it going to look when you're not even liking my pictures?"

"It's going to look like we're filming a video together! You know a thousand people are gonna watch it anyway —"

"And we should get a thousand more, but I get drop-offs when people stop liking my posts." Hailey wasn't exaggerating. She'd only gotten two offers from companies that week to promote their wares, and a photo of her breakfast that morning — an açaí bowl with homemade keto granola

— had gotten a hundred fewer likes than a similar photo the week before. Hailey worried that she'd only continue to fall.

Tom, though, wasn't worried at all — which bothered Hailey more than any lack of likes. "It doesn't matter," he said.

"It does! How does it look when my boyfriend doesn't like my posts, when he goes around liking everyone else's pictures and not mine?"

"No one cares!"

"Everyone cares!" Hailey sped towards Tom and grabbed his phone before he could react. "Everyone watches us, and everyone can see when you don't like my stuff."

"Give me my phone!" Tom wrestled with Hailey for the phone before she could get to her page from his account, where she planned to mass-like every post from the past week.

"They're not just hearts!" she continued. Hailey spun and yanked away from Tom, which caused him to stumble back. He began to fall, and Hailey sent him down faster by hitting him in the chest with his phone. "They're likes —"

Tom's head struck the coffee table. The glass top cracked but didn't shatter. Hailey yanked him up by his shoulders.

"And when you don't like my posts —" Hailey slammed his face against the iron corner of the table — "you bury me!"

Hailey slammed Tom's head against the table one last time, then threw his limp body against the wall. Blood smeared from his face onto the wall as he slid lifeless onto the floor.

Hailey stood still and waited for Tom to move. When he didn't, she walked to his body and placed her fingers against his neck. His heart didn't beat.

Hailey knew this was bad.

She also knew she was supposed to be live in ninety minutes.

She'd find a better way to deal with Tom later. For now, she rolled him into her bedroom and shoved him under the bed, careful to bend in his feet so his shoes wouldn't be visible. She cleaned the trail of blood leading to her room, then scrubbed the table and placed a colorful cloth mat over the crack in the glass. The wall would have to wait until she could buy paint. Wiping the blood would just make the stain worse.

Once she was done, she sat on the couch and tried to collect her bearings. Tom was dead. People would wonder where he was. People would ask about him. She wondered what she'd say when they noticed that Tom was no longer in her feed. Hailey wondered if she should begin scrubbing Tom from her profile now. She had relationship statuses to change, his accounts to unfollow.

But doing that now would only prompt more questions. Why had they disconnected? Did they break up? Where was Tom?

Hailey brought herself out of her thoughts, shook her head, and looked at her phone. She would have to buy time — and the best way was to act normal. She picked up her phone. She'd do her live episode without him. She had before. And before that, she'd post a selfie.

———————

"Hi everyone!" Hailey waved into the camera of her phone. Her laptop sat open beside her so she could monitor comments and likes on her feed while she recorded her Instagram Live on her phone. It was a lot of windows and a lot of people to watch, but Hailey was used to it. She smiled as she greeted her faceless followers. She couldn't see who she was waving to, but hearts began to swim around her face as her viewers liked that she was there.

"It's Thursday night," she continued. "And that means it's time to check in with you before my awesome weekend! As always, you can send me questions, and I'll answer them while I talk about what's been going on lately. So, yesterday I went to a really great sandwich shop in Dupont Circle, and —"

A question interrupted Hailey almost immediately. They always did, but while Hailey expected the question, it still caught her off-guard: *Where's Tom?*

Hailey smiled and looked back at her camera. "Someone's already asked me about Tom! He's not here tonight. He's out and about, but hopefully he'll be back for next week's video." She made a mental note to set the virtual stage for a dramatic exit on Tom's behalf, where, after months of love and joy and visiting the hottest places together, he'd straight-up ghost her. That was why he wasn't online through his various accounts: he was avoiding her. Maybe she'd get everyone to search for him. She tried not to chuckle at the thought of all of her followers going on a wild-goose chase for someone who was dead — nor frown at the thought of all of them flocking away from her feed in search of his.

A swarm of typed sighs and sad-face emojis came through, and Hailey sighed as she slumped her shoulders for effect. "I know, you guys, I miss him, too. But we'll see him and his beautiful face again soon."

Hailey heard a ding, which signaled that someone liked one of her previous posts. She looked at her laptop and checked which post it was as she continued to speak. "Anyway, this sandwich shop, Bahn Mots, is a Vietnamese fusion place which offers new takes on the classic —"

Hailey stopped as she checked her notifications. Her breakfast that morning, the one with fewer likes than the breakfast she'd posted before, had one new like — from TommyBoy89.

Hailey blinked, then refreshed the photo. She didn't see Tom's username, just the thousands of likes that had been there before.

Hailey ignored it. It was probably a mistake.

"Sorry guys," she said with a shrug. "I got distracted by someone liking my breakfast this morning. Did you all try that keto granola? I couldn't believe how good it was, especially since it didn't have any oats."

A flock of hearts flew through her screen. One follower wrote, *It looked so good! I'm making it tomorrow!* Another added, *I bet keto's why your face is so pretty.*

"Aw, thanks to the follower who said my face is pretty. It's just average, guys —" Hailey patted her cheeks as she looked from side to side — "and I keep it decent-looking with good food, good health, and this awesome oat scrub I just started using. It —"

Before Hailey could talk about the soap she'd promised the organic start-up she'd promote in exchange for free products and a boost on their channels, she got another like on an old post. It was a selfie she'd posted the day before to show off her new makeup, a blue eye shadow that Tom said made her eyes look like an autumn sky over her freckles. Hailey shared his comment in her post and tagged him, yet still, it had gone unliked.

Until now. TommyBoy89 liked the post.

"What the hell?" Hailey muttered. She didn't realize she'd spoken out loud until a series of questions came through from her followers, all various forms of *What?*

"Oh, nothing," Hailey replied with a smile, though it was weaker than it'd been before. "I just got distracted by another like on my makeup selfie from yesterday."

Another question came through, and Hailey readied a response on who the company was, or which colors would best suit which skin tones. The question, though, wasn't about her eye shadow. *Hey, sorry I'm late. Where's Tom?*

Hailey kept her smile, but sighed through it. She hoped it was quiet enough to not get picked up on the mic. "I just got another question about Tom," she said. She knew avoiding questions about him would cause more suspicion than ignoring them. "You all must really miss him!"

Another cluster of hearts swam across the screen, and Hailey tried not to glower at Tom's popularity. She and Tom were popular. That was what the hearts were for: the two of them.

"Like I said before, I don't know where he is tonight," Hailey said with as much enthusiasm as she could muster. "But hopefully we'll see him soon."

Hailey heard another ding. She closed her eyes at the sound. All she'd wanted when Tom was alive was just one heart, one like to show her he was watching her online. Now that he was dead, his hearts were all she heard — and they were the last thing she wanted.

The sound of a question made her open her eyes. She read: *What's wrong?*

Hailey smiled again. She had to remember she was live. "Nothing, sorry," she said. "I'm getting a lot of likes again. Now, this scrub."

Another ding. Another like. Hailey ignored it. She picked up the scrub and continued, "It's from a new company called Oatshine, and —"

*Ding.*

"They use all-organic oats and fruits —"

*Ding. Ding.*

"Which sounds like breakfast, and really, it is like breakfast, but for your —"

*Dingdingdingdingdingdingding* —

"WHAT?" Hailey slammed down the scrub and checked her notifications. She saw several likes, all of them for pictures she'd posted over the past six months — and all of them from TommyBoy89.

It couldn't be. Tom was dead beneath her bed, and his phone lay still on the coffee table next to her. Hailey checked each notification to see if he was indeed liking her pictures, but when she refreshed them, Tom's likes would disappear amongst the thousands of others, part of a number that Hailey lost count of within minutes of her pictures going viral.

But as he had in life, Tom stood out from the rest. His username clamored for her attention as she tried to keep up with his hearts. The likes became a steady beat that Hailey knew she'd have to ignore. "It's a soap I've started using every day, and if you use the code HailStorm20, you'll get twenty percent off your first order."

The dings ceased. Hailey sighed with relief. "Now, this weekend," she continued. "I've got a lot of fun stuff planned —"

A follower asked her a question: *Didn't you have some big announcement with Tom?*

Hailey's grin stayed frozen in place as she replied, "Some of you remember that Tom and I were going to have a big announcement tonight." How could they forget? She'd talked about it for a week to get their followers excited. She'd talked about it, but Tom had not. Tom had posted pictures of his dinner, a couple selfies with her, and only one picture of her the night before, with a caption saying he'd have something special to share about a special someone very soon. It'd gotten lots of likes. So had Hailey's announcements — but not one like from him. Hailey seethed a little as she continued, "But, as I've mentioned a couple times now, he's not here; and I don't want to say anything without him."

Another ding, a single one this time. Hailey forgot her followers as she opened the picture that was liked. It was a close-up she'd taken of Tom after one month of dating, one that emphasized his eyes. The same beautiful eyes she'd seen when she clicked through to his profile all those months ago. Hailey bit her lip and tried not to hyperventilate despite her heartbeat climbing in time with her notifications. The thrum of dings thrashed in her ears as she stared at him staring at her.

One of her viewers asked, *What's wrong?*

"N-nothing," Hailey replied, though she couldn't smile.

*You look awful,* another follower wrote.

*Eat more açaí bowls,* a third one quipped.

A swarm of hearts flooded the screen. Hailey knew they weren't for her, but for the viewer's joke. She furrowed her brow and said as calmly as she could, "Really, I'm okay."

*Ding. Ding. Ding.*

"I'm just ready for the weekend, and —"

*Ready for Tom to come back?*

Hailey paused, then said, "Yes." She took a breath as she composed herself. A little vulnerability would only make her story about being ghosted all the more tragic. "Yes, I'm more than ready to see him again. I miss him, even though it's only been a short while since I've —"

A ding snapped in her ears, and she looked at her laptop before she could stop herself. She clicked through when she saw that the notification wasn't just a like, but a comment. Hailey saw the first picture they'd taken together, one she'd snapped the afternoon after their first date. Tom kissed her cheek and she grinned at the camera. Underneath the picture, TommyBoy89 had written, *Hi.*

Hailey covered her mouth and tried not to scream. The dings became a steady stream once more — *dingdingdingding-dingdingding* — and she moved her hands to her ears to quiet their call. A question popped up on her screen and glared her in the eye: *Yeah, where's Tom?*

Their questions had to stop. Tom's likes had to stop. Tom had to be stopped. She'd stopped him before, and everyone would see it and know that they should stop, too, before she lost her mind.

"You want to know where Tom is?" Hailey snapped.

She jumped up and stormed into her bedroom. Hailey dragged his body from beneath the bed and wrapped her arm around his shoulder to steady him as she held up her phone. "Here he is! Here's Tom! So stop asking me, stop asking where he is, and for God's sake —" she stared into his open, lifeless eyes and his bloodied, broken face — "STOP LIKING MY PICS!"

# PERFECTION IN SHADOW

Colin never thought he'd find the perfect woman. Everyone he met had something wrong with them once sex and passion ran their course. They talked too much. They took up too much space. Their looks were harsh under the light.

His girlfriend left him in a huff after their latest fight. The sound of the door slamming behind her reverberated through the apartment. Colin swore he saw the shadows tremble beneath its echo across the floor. He wondered how the floor would move if he instead buried her beneath it.

The darkness trembled. Colin blinked, then saw the shadows fall back into place.

He thought of his girlfriend — now his ex — meeting other men. He thought of her going to bed with them. She'd been so eager to jump into bed with him. She'd do the same with any stranger who showed an interest.

The shadow arched back and sighed. Before reason could stop him, Colin moved to the shadow and caressed it. The shadow leaned into his palm and smiled.

Colin smiled back. Here was the secret. Here was what he needed to do to keep someone.

Piece by piece, Colin took the darkest corners of his fantasies and made the perfect woman. He imagined slapping one, and a face turned and looked away. He imagined gripping one against him, and a body stood slack and still, waiting to be held. Finally, he imagined telling every woman he knew to shut up.

A shadow stood silent in his window, a beautiful woman who was perfect for him. One made of his darkness — one that wouldn't disappear from him.

Colin walked to her and touched her shoulder. She didn't tremble. She didn't speak.

"You're perfect," he whispered.

She turned and wrapped her arms around him, creating a shroud that consumed him. Before he could scream, Colin felt a coldness clench his throat and seep through his veins as he disappeared into darkness.

The apartment lay empty. A single ray of light shined through the window.

# SALT

They called me at 5:30 in the morning. I was making a pot of coffee for one. Something told me even before they called that I wouldn't need to make him coffee today.

Something changes in the air when you know something, especially about someone you love. You can feel their mood even when they don't say a word, can feel it in your heart when something has happened to them even when they're not there to tell you. I knew when the phone rang that someone was going to tell me about John, and that it wasn't going to be John who did the telling.

"Mrs. Carson?" A monotone voice, likely tired from the night shift, floated into my ear.

"Yes?" I replied. "What is it?" I asked, even though I knew, in the way that only a wife can know, that it was about John.

———

"Excuse me."

I looked up from my drink and saw a pair of eyes that matched the bottle of Bombay Sapphire glowing on the shelf behind the bar. The bartender smiled at me and pointed at my near-empty glass. "Can I top you off?" he asked as he held up a bottle of Grey Goose.

I smiled back and held out my glass. The vodka splashed over my crushed slice of lime and partially melted ice. "I didn't have Grey Goose, though," I admitted as he poured. "Just Absolut."

"I know. I saw your tab." He winked as he ended the pour. "Consider it on the house."

A small wave rushed from my hips to between my thighs — one that I knew would land me in someone's bed, or at least someone's arms, if I had the courage to see it through. I studied his face, his cheeks covered with speckles of black stubble, a brown mop of hair hanging over his forehead. He wore a white t-shirt and jeans, as if bartending in the neon glow of an overpriced bar in Farragut North were the most casual thing in the world. His sense of ease reached across the bar and touched me. I longed to feel his touch in other ways.

"Thank you." I pressed my mouth around my straw — delicately, just enough to have the straw rest in proposition against my bottom lip. I saw him try not to notice. "I don't accept free drinks from strangers, though," I said with a grin.

"Probably smart," he said with a mischievous glint in his eyes. He leaned forward and dropped a fresh slice of lime into my glass. "I'm John."

―――――――

"I'm sorry to tell you all this, Mrs. Carson," the officer continued. "I know this can't be easy."

"It isn't," I replied.

"I'm sure this is a shock for you."

"It is. I didn't suspect a thing." Because that's what you're supposed to say, all that you can really say, when someone calls you and says that your husband has been arrested for murder.

———

The sex was ferocious. It wasn't the night we met — he had a late shift, and I wanted our first night together to be a whole night together. We met up the next night, when he wasn't scheduled to work. We had the fastest dinner I'd ever consumed, then hurried to my apartment, tearing off each other's clothes the minute my door clicked shut.

His fingers moved over me as deftly as they'd done over the bins of limes and olives at the bar. He kissed my breasts, my stomach, my mound. He hadn't shaved, and I relished the friction of his stubble all over my body. His lips made his way back up to mine, and I held him by his hair as he sucked and bit my bottom lip.

His excitement got the better of him. His teeth sunk into the flesh behind my lip, and I tasted blood before I yelped. He pulled back, a mix of alarm and apology on his face. Both disappeared when I smiled and licked the blood from my lip. I swallowed, then brought him back in for a kiss, let him taste the salt left behind from what he'd done to me.

He grinned and kissed me back, biting more gently this time, running his tongue across my own. Both of us relishing our lust for each other, our lust for blood.

———

I'd have to go to the police soon. I'd have to see if there was any way that I could get my husband back.

In that moment, though, all I could see was an empty kitchen. I blinked back tears as I thought of the morning ahead. Before I'd even had an inkling that I would be alone, I'd thought of making breakfast for the two of us, John back from his night shift with meat for the skillet, me making eggs and toast to go with it. John had left me a supply. I wouldn't go hungry without him, and I could replenish my stock even if he were gone.

I choked back a sob as it began to settle in. Gone.

————

I had many appetites, most insatiable, and most that I kept to myself until I met John. As we grew closer, I told him everything I longed for. He did his best to grant my wishes, even though he himself was an answer to my prayers. I loved the mischief in his eyes, the predatory glint in his smile, the look he gave me when he was ready to devour me in bed.

When we were married in the courthouse, a modest ceremony to pledge our devotion, he promised me he'd take care of me, that he'd satisfy my deepest desires. He filled that promise by giving himself to me.

That didn't stop me from taking him up on his offer to keep me sated.

————

A single beep told me that my cup of coffee was ready. I ignored it as I stared at the contents of our freezer, filled to the brim with the fruits of John's labors. Everything John had brought home for me when he completed the night shift.

Arms and legs were stacked on one another, purple and blue from being frozen. Hands with nails removed and fingers severed sat stacked in sandwich baggies, sealed tight to keep them safe from freezer burn. Other parts looked more like blobs without the context of the bodies they came from, but I knew them well. Breasts and stomachs (too fatty, but good for stews). Cheeks (only from the face). Never feet. I hated feet, even when John jokingly offered to pickle them.

I always liked fresh meat better, but even at my hungriest, I could never finish an entire body John brought home. Our freezer held the last of him, the last of what he'd ever give to me.

He hadn't gone to trial yet. It was possible he wouldn't be found guilty. I'd have to burn the fruits of his labors before any police officers arrived. I'd have to dispose of his gifts somehow.

A tear trickled into the corner of my mouth. I tasted salt on my tongue. I remembered the sting of John's bite, the salt of John's fingertips. I'd give up my bounty for John. I'd take care of it all after breakfast — the meal I'd suspected, in the way that only a wife could know, that I would be eating alone. I grabbed one last baggie of fingers out of the freezer and placed a skillet on the stove.

# SEED

Aidy woke up with warmth on her skin. Part of it came from the sunbeam through the window, but most of it came from the feel of her boyfriend Jake sleeping next to her. She smiled as she woke him up through touch: her lips on his cheek, her fingers on his waist, her toes on the hairs of his leg as she rubbed her foot along his calf. "Good morning," she said.

"Morning," Jake mumbled as he pulled her close. She ran her fingers through his hair and began to kiss him, a kiss she had no intention of ending at his lips. They were interrupted, though, when her fingers touched a foreign object in his hair.

"You were up late in the yard again, weren't you?" Aidy said as she plucked a dead leaf from Jake's hair.

"Just checking for weeds," Jake said with a shrug.

"I've never known anyone who gardened by moonlight."

"Gotta do it sometime when I go to work early and get home late."

"You should start leaving a comb with your garden supplies so you can get rid of any stray plants wandering inside with you," Aidy said as she crumpled the leaf into fragments in her fingers.

"That reminds me — I need some supplies." Jake swung his feet to the floor and Aidy furrowed her brow.

"Are you serious? Now?"

"I like to beat the suburbia crowd at Home Depot. You know that." Jake pulled on a pair of jeans and a t-shirt. Aidy grew more disappointed with each article of clothing that covered his body.

"I also know we were going to start the morning a little more slowly," she said with as good of a seductive purr as she could manage, given her voice was still thick with sleep, and the remnants of the night were starting to build on her teeth and in her breath.

"How about this —" Jake walked over to her and sat on the bed. "I'll go as fast as I can, and when I get back, we'll go as slow as we want to."

"I'd like that." Aidy smiled as Jake kissed her cheek. He stood up before she could pull him close and try one last time to keep him in bed for a little longer.

"See you soon," Jake called as he walked out of their room.

"Bye," Aidy called back.

The door slammed shut in response. Aidy wondered if he'd even heard her, or if his head was already too occupied with yard work. She turned and fell back asleep.

In what felt like a moment, she awoke to the sound of their front door opening. Aidy figured Jake couldn't wait, and rose to greet him. She walked into the hall, ready to embrace him and pick up where he'd left off.

Aidy turned the corner towards their living room and froze. The door lay in fragments, its pieces dwarfed by a cluster of vines that surged through the house.

———

*Days feel like moments when everything is gone.*

Aidy ran her fingertips across the words she'd scratched into a log the week before. Or perhaps it was the day before. It was hard to keep track, even with the tally marks she'd scratched into the log that once lay in their yard, waiting to be chopped into firewood.

The yard was still there. It just could hardly be called a yard when all that surrounded Aidy were trees that touched the sky, vines along the ground, grass that reached her waist, and dirt paths connecting them all.

All that time ago, Aidy's row house had been obliterated beneath the plants. The house and its neighbors were entombed in vines that became leafy mountains, ones that no one dared to climb. Aidy had been lucky enough to escape through a window before the vines could wrap around her and choke her, like the neighbors whose remains she saw before they'd been swallowed by mushrooms.

Her city — and, Aidy presumed, others — turned into a forest, one that trembled with danger as the breeze flowed through the leaves and all noises were hushed in the foliage. Everyone who survived the initial onslaught of the plants began to set up camp. Survivors called it the Growth whenever they talked about the forest that slowly consumed their livelihood each day. Large groups huddled around fires and hacked at the plants. Vines snuffed the fires and snapped the people up one by one.

The groups became pairs. The forest continued to grow.

Aidy had paired with her neighbor down the street, one that she'd only nodded at in passing while jogging or walking to her car in her life before the Growth. Her neighbor, whose name was Theresa, had been one of those survivalist types who did intense workouts and whose idea of fun was learning how to survive in the woods with nothing but string and a pen knife. Theresa told Aidy all about it the first day they paired up. Aidy didn't join Theresa for her daily workouts, but she was happy to learn how to forage and make a fire.

Even so, Theresa usually made the fires (she'd grow impatient when Aidy would try), and in return, Aidy brought food. At night, Theresa would smoke by the fire and eat berries with a frown. Aidy would sit with her for warmth and the occasional drag.

"Chris isn't dead," Theresa said one night. Aidy tried to remember what Theresa's husband had looked like, but she'd only ever seen him before the Growth — and even then, she'd only seen the back of his head as he got into his car.

"I saw him," Theresa continued. "He wasn't crushed or choked like everyone else who's died in this thing." She crushed her cigarette with trembling hands, and spat in the dirt towards a dandelion that had sprouted from the ground. "He always had dirt on his nails, seeds burrowed in his palm, leaves on his clothes …"

Aidy remembered the leaf she'd plucked from Jake's hair, and closed her eyes.

"Then one morning, I saw him walking into the forest, and he was covered in leaves. Head to toe. Looked like Swamp Thing, or like he was in some kind of camo." Theresa chuckled, but her laughter was soaked with unshed tears. "Except it wasn't like camo, because it looked like it was a part of him. Like the leaves and vines were his skin and his hair. He'd become like them." Theresa looked up, and Aidy could see the sorrow in her eyes in the light of the waning fire. "Or maybe they'd made him like them."

Aidy also suspected that Jake hadn't died. She hadn't found his body amongst the others she'd seen in the first days after the Growth. At first, she thought she'd find him in a group, but when days went by with no sign of him, she suspected that he'd just disappeared, whether on foot or by vanishing in a way she couldn't explain. The closest she'd come to an explanation had been a feeling she'd had when she'd walked by a tall, vine-covered tree awash in new leaves. Her heart beat a little faster, and in her mind, she heard his name.

She'd shaken off the feeling, figuring it was just her grief playing tricks on her memories. But she couldn't shake the feeling that Jake had vanished into the forest in ways that the other corpses had not. When she heard Theresa's story, she suspected that Chris met the same fate.

"You probably think it's crazy," Theresa said. "Everyone else did. They'd tell me Chris is dead and that I had to accept it. I know he's gone, but I also know what I saw. And I bet other people are becoming like them too, like the plants."

"Why?" Aidy asked. She didn't feel ready to share her thoughts on Jake. Even with Theresa's story, she wasn't sure if what she believed, what she felt, was in fact true.

Theresa shrugged. "Who knows? Why is the forest taking over? Why are we being hunted by what we used to gather? Why are some people killed and others spared, even though we're surrounded by plants that could snap at any moment?"

"Maybe to keep us on our toes."

Theresa breathed out a laugh. "My guess is the plants know that piling up the forest with dead bodies is too much for the ecosystem. Maybe turning a few of us into them will help them grow more than eating us all until there's no one left."

"I bet the mushrooms would have something to say about that."

"If a debate between mushrooms and vines about what to do with the humans was the craziest thing to come out of the Growth, we'd all be blessed." Theresa stood up and doused the last few flames with a can of water. She walked off without a word — she simply waved good night.

Aidy thought about Theresa's theories. She never had the chance to discuss them further with Theresa, or to tell her she suspected that Jake had met Chris' fate. Aidy came to her fire pit the next evening, and there was enough light on the ground for Aidy to see the tracks of dragged fingers leading from Theresa's canopy into the depths of the forest.

The solitary pairs became single people. The forest grew massive. Now, Aidy only had moments — moments carved into a log in jagged marks.

————

Aidy hadn't seen another person in several marks. She was fine with that. Large groups attracted the attention of the vines. Pairs meant friends she never saw again.

Still, Aidy couldn't deny that even with the overwhelming feeling of just wanting to stay alive, she felt a little lonely.

More than lonely or scared, though, she was hungry. Aidy hiked along the myriad paths threading through the forest. Fruit grew in numbers that were enough to feed what people were left. Aidy wondered if that was a fluke on the forest's part, or perhaps an act of mercy to keep them alive — charity on behalf of a tyrant that was just enough to fool people into thinking he was a benevolent king.

Aidy added pears to her basket, picking as many as she could. While there were still fish in the streams and greens interspersed with the plants, fruit was abundant in the forest, and fruit was what she preferred. What she couldn't eat, she managed to ferment into a cider that helped the nights feel a little less lonely.

The sound of a crack in the distance caught her attention. Aidy looked up and expected to see vines that had decided to do away with her at last. However, she saw nothing — no vines, and no animals.

*Crack.* Aidy moved a little closer to the sound. If it was an animal, perhaps she could try to hunt it for food. She reached the clearing and stopped when she saw the source of the sound: a man.

Aidy hadn't seen the man before — and she knew she would've remembered seeing him, even within the larger groups. He was tall, and had hair the color of amber that fell over his ears in wisps curled by the humidity. His skin was the color of honey, probably tanned from living outdoors. He was kind enough to leave a good portion of his skin visible, courtesy of an unbuttoned flannel shirt with cut-off sleeves. His arms poured out of his sleeves, and his lean muscles curved and stretched as he looked for food.

Aidy wondered if he'd been flung from his home like everyone else, or if he'd been birthed from a tree while covered in golden tears of myrrh. She felt a rush of tingles settle between her thighs as she watched him gather berries. She remembered something other than cider that could make the nights feel a little less lonely — something she hadn't thought of since before the Growth.

A slithering sound stopped her thoughts. She saw four large vines shoot towards the man. She remembered everything and everyone they'd taken away, including Theresa and Jake. She swallowed a small lump that formed in her throat. After all the vines had done, it was only natural they'd take away her first source of feeling in days.

The man pivoted just as the vines were a foot away from him. He dropped his basket and, in one swift motion, withdrew a machete and hacked the closest vine. He made three more chops, and Aidy swore she heard a hiss as the sliced pieces of vine curled back into the grass. One slithered in her direction, and Aidy hopped onto a rock.

The vine paid her no mind, crawling past her like a snake in retreat. She looked back towards the man. He wiped his machete with the bottom of his shirt. The blade dripped with green ooze that was as thick as blood. Aidy wondered if their appetite for people was making the vines bleed like animals.

The man took off his shirt and scrunched it into his back pocket, the bloodied end hanging from him like a tail. Aidy stopped thinking about the plants entirely. She studied his back. The lines of his muscles looked like roots that moved up his back and down his waist. Aidy found herself wanting to touch the roots, to follow them wherever they led and to trace the tree that was etched into his body.

He looked up as he returned the machete to its sheath, and happened to glance in her direction. Aidy knew he'd seen her even before his eyebrows raised upward. Before he could speak, Aidy jumped down and hurried away. She wasn't ready to speak to someone, to grow close to someone she'd eventually lose — even if that someone made her feel a warmth that stayed with her long after he was out of sight.

Back at her canopy, Aidy couldn't stop thinking about the man. She played the image of him walking through the foliage over and over again in her mind. Sometimes she was so overcome that she'd sit still and close her eyes, doing nothing but remembering his golden skin and his wispy hair. She ate pears and thought of him licking the juice that dripped between her breasts. She bathed in the creek and thought of him holding her in the water and kissing her neck and her shoulders.

That night, Aidy touched herself in the quiet of the forest. She lay on the dirt beneath her canopy and imagined the man above her. She imagined tracing the lines along his back as her fingertips pressed her clitoris and stroked her mound. A ripple began to form that she hadn't felt since Jake disappeared. It crept from her hips and spread to her toes and her lips. She knew she should be quiet, but the ripple begged to be released. Her mouth dropped open, and a small moan came out before she could stop it.

Aidy heard a rustle of leaves close by. She stopped, snapped her mouth closed, and lay still.

Nothing appeared — no vines, no leaves. The rustling stopped.

The tingling, though, did not. Aidy continued her fantasy, rubbing herself until she came to climax. Aidy knew better than to cry out. It could bring a ravenous vine to her tent. Instead, she closed her eyes and opened her mouth, her cry a silent sigh that moved in time with a breeze blowing through the grass.

———

Pleasuring herself, along with a good night's rest, helped to temper Aidy's desire for the man she'd seen. She was able to go about her day and not be overcome by thoughts of him. Those thoughts were there, though, flickering in and out of her conscious as she cleaned the dirt from her fingernails, fished in the stream, cleaned the bass she caught, and cooked it for dinner along with some dandelion greens.

She watched the sunset as she swallowed her last bite of food. It was a beautiful evening, pink and red and orange, like scoops of sherbet over the cones of the shadowed trees. Her dinner, while simple, satisfied her stomach. The meal and the sky both would've been better with someone to share them with.

Aidy shook her head. It wouldn't be better. The sky and the meal couldn't hide the fact that she was in the forest because the forest wanted to consume everyone in its path. At least when the forest finally came for her, she'd be alone.

Aidy picked up her cider. Before she could drink it, she saw an orange glow emerge in the distance. A campfire — and where there was fire, there was people. Aidy stood up, ready to go see who had lit it.

She stopped herself. She'd sworn off pairs after Theresa was killed. It wasn't worth growing close to someone when everyone would be gone eventually, whether dragged off like Theresa or turned into foliage like Jake.

She watched the orange glow for a few moments longer. She looked at the sunset, which had turned purple and blue with the coming night. She thought of how she'd watched it alone, just like she'd eaten alone, and just like she'd die alone. She thought of the rush she'd felt when she saw the man, saw a person, for the first time in days. For a moment at least, loneliness didn't seem so appealing.

Aidy decided to seize that moment.

---

The sound of the fire crackling grew louder as Aidy neared its glow. She reached the clearing and slowed her gait, not wanting to startle the person there. "Hello?" she called — softly, so as not to attract any plants, but loud enough for the person to hopefully hear.

She heard no answer. Aidy wondered if the person was gone. She moved closer to the fire and stopped when she saw a shadow move across the ground.

The shadow stopped. Aidy heard a voice say, "Hello?"

She looked up and saw the man from the forest standing by the fire. Aidy tried not to stare, even though he was in the same unbuttoned shirt and still had the same wisps of hair curling over his ears — and now, he had a smile to add to the mix that sent her heart into a spin.

"You're the woman who ran away yesterday," he said.

Aidy smiled a little, and hoped she wouldn't blush. "I didn't want to —"

"Run into any more vines?"

"Well, you did a pretty good job fending them off."

"I do what I can." He patted the machete, which was in a sheathe attached to his khaki shorts. "Seems like you do too, since you're still alive."

"I just try to avoid them and not make too much noise."

The fire popped, which startled them both. The man smiled again, and said, "So, do you want me to turn down the volume on the fire or something?"

"No," Aidy replied with a chuckle. "I was just ... it was the first fire I'd seen in weeks. You're the first person I've seen in weeks. I wanted to check it out, see who you were."

"Well, I'm Evan, and I've been in this part of the forest for about three days."

"This part? You've been traveling?"

"You try not to make too much noise, I try not to stay in one place for too long." Evan nodded towards the fire. "I was just about to have some berries for dessert. Want to join me?"

She did. Aidy sat across from Evan on the ground, and slowly ate a large handful of raspberries while they talked by the fire. They didn't talk about their lives before the Growth, but how they'd survived since. Evan spoke of moving from group to group, then clearing to clearing, in the twenty miles and several days between his former home and where he was now. Aidy listened with interest, and also with appreciation for the mellow timber of his voice, which was as warm as the fire they sat beside.

"Wandering isn't so bad," Evan said as he licked raspberry juice from his fingertips. "But I won't lie — sometimes I miss my living room."

"I hear that." Aidy sighed as she thought about her couch, and how soft its cushions were compared to mud and grass. "I miss being inside. I miss watching TV." She chuckled sadly. "TV. Everything we've lost, and I miss TV."

"There's nothing wrong with that." Evan smiled as he leaned over his knees. Doing so brought an orange glow to his eyes. Aidy tried not to get distracted. "I miss Snickers bars. Not just food — well, food that isn't fruit or fish or squirrels —"

"You've caught squirrels? Lucky bastard."

"Maybe one in the last month. But I'd trade all of those for one Snickers bar."

"I'd give up all the pear cider I've made for one more concert. A good one, outdoors with beer and hot dogs and music that makes my ears ring."

"Who'd be the headliner?"

"Oh Christ, I can't pick —"

"Just the first band that comes to mind. Count of three: one, two, three."

"Britney Spears."

"Britney?" Evan laughed, and Aidy put her face in her hands, though with a smile. "You want a pop concert?"

"Like that wouldn't be a great show."

"You know what, it would. I'd love to see Britney Spears." Evan leaned back and sighed happily. "A nice pop concert under the stars."

"That would be nice."

Evan smiled at her, and Aidy smiled back. She hadn't felt this happy in a long time.

"I've also missed this," Aidy said. "Just talking."

Evan nodded. "One downside to wandering around has been a lack of conversation — well, with people other than myself and some unlucky squirrels."

"But even with other people, all we've talked about was the Growth, or finding food, or staying safe, or just — just everything terrible. I've missed talking about nothing. I've missed dreaming about silly things. I've missed talking about pleasures, you know?"

"Yeah. Yeah, I do." Evan's smile softened, and he looked Aidy in the eye. "Though I didn't realize how much I missed that until I talked to you."

Aidy did her best to not look down or blush, or to curl her toes at the growing warmth she felt from his gaze. She'd missed the pleasure of someone's company, company that wasn't just for survival.

What she hadn't missed, though, was the feeling of loss that came when someone disappeared. Evan didn't seem to be in danger of disappearing, but that was the trouble with life after the Growth: no one knew when someone else would wilt.

"Well, thank you for the raspberries," Aidy said as she stood up. "And the conversation."

"You're leaving?" Evan asked with a furrowed brow.

"It's late, and —"

"It's not like we have work tomorrow. Don't tell me you miss that."

"In a funny way, I do." Aidy laughed a little, and Evan walked towards her. Aidy stood still, even though she knew with each step closer he took, it'd be harder for her to leave.

Evan stood a few inches away from her. His fingers moved towards her wrist, then stopped. Aidy made no effort to move her hand away. She moved it in front of her, in plain sight and willing to be touched if he so chose. Part of her knew she shouldn't stay, but another part of her ached so much to feel him that even just his fingertips would satisfy her.

"You sure you don't want to stay a little longer?" Evan asked. He gently touched her wrist, and it took all of Aidy's strength to not shudder with pleasure beneath his touch. His fingers were callused, but they still felt soothing and warm upon her skin. Aidy imagined his fingers traveling up her arm to her neck, with his lips close behind. Aidy had a feeling he would follow through on her fantasy if she asked him to.

A separate feeling disrupted her fantasy: a bump on Evan's hand. His palm had made its way to her wrist, and Aidy felt tiny pebbles upon it. Aidy looked at his palm, and saw a cluster of seeds in the crease. They could've been from the ground, or even the raspberries. But they also could've been a part of him, the beginnings of him turning into the plants that consumed them.

Aidy jumped and snapped her hand back before she could stop herself. She took a breath to calm her fearful thoughts. She glanced at Evan, and her fear was replaced with shame when she saw how wounded he looked.

"I'm sorry," Evan said. "I —"

"Oh, no, don't be," Aidy replied. "I didn't mind, I just —"

"You said you wanted to go, and I should've let you. I will."

Aidy didn't want him to. She didn't want to leave.

A breeze blew through the leaves, and the rustling noise reminded her that she had to. It didn't matter what they wanted — their fate was up to the Growth.

"It's just been a long day," Aidy said. She knew her excuse sounded weak to anyone with deductive listening skills, but still, she held to it. "And I'm tired."

"I understand." He gave a small smile, which comforted her. "Well, you know where to find me if you want some company again."

"Right." Aidy waved. "Have a good night."

"You too. Hope to see you soon."

Aidy nodded, then turned and left, forcing herself to not look back at him.

———

Aidy woke up the next morning and promised herself a day of solitude. She needed to forget how nice Evan's company had felt — and if she couldn't do that, she at least needed to remind herself that being alone felt just as good.

She went through her daily routine since the Growth. She looked for fruit, and caught two fish in the stream — one for lunch and one for dinner, not one for him and one for her. She bathed in the lake and took extra care to wash under her arms and her breasts, reaching the places where sweat liked to hide — so she would be comfortable, not so she would smell nice in case he held her later.

As Aidy ate her dinner by a small fire, she found herself looking past the clearing. She saw no orange glow in the distance.

Good. It gave her no reason to go looking for company.

She watched the stars and drank a cup of pear cider. She wondered what Evan was doing.

She finished her cider, then looked in the direction of his clearing. Nothing.

She doused the fire, then curled up under her canopy and went to sleep. She did her best not to dream of him.

Her dreams did not cooperate. Aidy saw Evan in flashes as she slept — touching her breasts, kissing her shoulders, nestling between her legs as she guided him into her. Aidy woke up bothered throughout the night. After the third time, she crossed her legs and squeezed until the sensation abetted. As she went back to sleep, her mind conjured one last fantasy of falling asleep in his arms.

When she next awoke, the sun was up. Aidy ate two pears for breakfast and found herself looking in the direction of Evan's clearing. Her mind didn't tell her to stay put. She felt no urge to be alone. She'd spent all of the day before alone. She'd spent several days alone, days she thought were better than the ones she'd shared with others.

They weren't better — at least, not better than time that she could spend with Evan.

Aidy walked towards Evan's clearing with a determined stride. She'd talk to him. She'd see if he wanted to have dinner later. She'd be his neighbor. She didn't know if they would be more, but she would accept just being more than alone in the woods.

She stopped when she reached the clearing. Evan wasn't there.

His canopy was empty. She thought she saw footprints leading away, but they weren't fresh. Leaves filled their gaps. She searched the ground for tracks left by fingers, or any sign of blood.

She shook her head. Evan hadn't been taken away, like Theresa. He hadn't disappeared like Chris or Jake. He might have, but she didn't know for sure. He was just away.

He was just gone.

Aidy swallowed and tried not to cry at the thought of losing someone else, someone she'd barely even formed any memories of before they'd gone away.

"Aidy?"

The sound of his voice was better than anything she'd heard since the Growth. She turned and saw Evan walk into the clearing. He held a small rope bag full of apples, and smiled when he saw her, albeit with curiosity. "What are you doing here?" he asked.

"I …" Aidy tried to steady her voice. She didn't want him to see how scared she'd been that he was gone, or how relieved she was that he was there. "I wanted to see if you wanted to have breakfast," she said.

"I've actually eaten. I got these for later." He held up the apples as he spoke. "There's a whole bunch of apple trees about five miles from here. I found them yesterday."

"Yesterday?"

"Yeah, I wandered pretty far — so far that I ended up sleeping out that way. I lost track of time before it got dark." He smiled. "Not sure if you came by for dessert again, but if you did, that's where I was."

"I didn't," Aidy said with a laugh, though it was shaky. "Were you that desperate for apples or something?"

Evan's smile became sheepish. "The apples were happenstance, but … well, I was actually looking for squirrels. I was going to catch one for you, see if you wanted one for dinner."

Aidy became too overwhelmed to speak.

"I didn't find any," Evan added with a shrug. "But at least I found some apples, something to break up the raspberries and — hey." Evan set down the bag and his machete as Aidy looked away, her face in her palm. "Hey, what's wrong?"

Aidy shook her head. "Nothing."

"What's the matter?"

"It's nothing, really."

"Look, I'll be honest: squirrels don't taste that good. You're not missing much."

Aidy laughed, one that was less shaky than before. She saw Evan smiling at her. It gave her enough confidence to finally say out loud, "I thought you were gone."

"Gone? I mean yeah, I was away —"

"Gone for good. I didn't see your campfire last night, and I didn't see you this morning, and ..." She looked at the ground as he moved towards her. "I feel so stupid," she whispered.

"Don't," he said in a low, soothing voice. He touched her shoulder. "It makes sense you'd think that after everything that's happened."

Evan squeezed her shoulder and ran his fingers in circles on her skin. Aidy leaned her head on his shoulder before she realized what she was doing. She was about to lift it, until Evan wrapped his arms around her and held her close. She sighed as she buried her face into his shoulder, and tried not to breathe too deeply as she smelled his musk, a pleasant scent of sweet fruit, pine, and salt.

"So many people have disappeared," she said. "I've spent so much time by myself, and just when I thought I didn't want to be alone anymore ..."

"I know. But I'm here."

Aidy closed her eyes as she took in the feel of his body against hers. She wrapped her arms around his waist, felt his back beneath her palms. She wanted so badly to run her fingers up and down his bare back, find the lines she'd seen the other day and trace them over and over.

Evan held her more tightly. His fingers traced the small of her back. He nestled his cheek against her hair, fell a little into her hold in a way that suggested surrender. She heard him take a deep breath, and Aidy's heart picked up speed.

Aidy felt Evan catch himself. She remembered her reaction the other night, and decided to let him know just how much she enjoyed his touch. How much she wanted to feel him beneath her, beside her, all over her.

She pressed him closer to her, then slowly ran her fingers beneath the bottom of his shirt. Evan sighed, and Aidy felt him shudder; but both were done with pleasure. She found the lines of his back with her fingertips and traced upward, following the path from the small of his back to his shoulders.

Evan nestled his head into the nape of her neck and pulled her closer. He lifted one hand and ran his fingers through her hair. "It's been so long since I've held someone," he whispered, his breath warm in her ear.

It'd been so long for Aidy too — too long. She moved her fingers up and down his back, smooth and free of seeds or leaves. There was only his skin and a few beads of sweat. There was only Evan. There was only the two of them.

Aidy opened her eyes. Her gaze fell on the clearing. All was quiet except for Evan's sigh as his lips moved from her ear to her neck. All was still except for their hands — and a quiet, creeping cluster of vines that slid in silence from the tall grass surrounding them.

Aidy stopped her tracing and gripped Evan's back. Evan lifted his head, but looked at her instead of behind them. "What's —"

Evan didn't get a chance to ask. Aidy pushed him aside, her gaze fixed on the thin, flowered tendrils moving towards them. The vines had had their fun. The vines had destroyed her life, had claimed Jake for their own and taken Theresa for their food. They'd left her alive, but taken root in her brain and let her know that they would come for her whenever she felt a brief moment of happiness, when she wasn't thinking of them and instead thinking of her own pleasure, her own means of living well for however much longer she had to live.

Aidy was over it.

She grabbed Evan's machete and hacked four small vines at once. Four more, then three, then two. Their shorn pieces lay limp, the flowers on the vines beginning to wilt; and the other halves began to retreat. Aidy followed them, hacking them into pieces as they shuffled back into the clearing.

The flowers disappeared, and a large, thick, bristled vine seeped through the grass. It looked like an overgrown garden slug, like the kind Jake would pluck gently from his flower beds. "Some people kill them with salt," he'd explained. "But I'd rather steer them away. They're just hungry."

Aidy wasn't Jake. She lifted the machete over her head, then swung it down over the vine with all of her anger. She swung for Jake, for Theresa, even for Evan, who was stuck wandering an overgrown forest in fear for his life from a swarm of angry, ravenous plants. She chopped the vine over and over, and stopped when nothing else came through the clearing. The vine lay in pieces that wilted and oozed into the dirt .

"Jesus," Evan breathed.

Aidy turned and saw Evan standing in shock where she'd left him. "I would've helped," he added. "But honestly, I didn't want to get in the line of fire."

Aidy chuckled, then speared a piece of the vine with the machete. "You helped by providing the weapon," she said as she held the machete up, the vine shining in the sun as green slime dripped to the ground.

"You should set that up like a stake. A warning to other —"

Evan stopped speaking in time with Aidy dropping the machete to the ground. Her eyes fixed on his as she strode back over to him. The vines, and her fear, were both gone. All Aidy felt was the desire she'd had before they were interrupted

— and she wasn't going to ignore it. Aidy hooked her fingers through Evan's belt loops and pulled him into a deep, fervent kiss.

Their hands moved up and down each other's bodies to get a sense of what they were about to explore. Evan slid his tongue into her mouth, and Aidy groaned as he held her tighter and tangled his fingers in her hair. They kissed over and over with growing speed. Evan let go of Aidy only to allow her to slide his shirt off of his arms.

Aidy kissed his neck, shoulders, and chest as she ran her fingers up and down his back. She felt every line, felt his skin grow warm beneath her touch and light the way for her fingers to reach his belt and his fly. Both came undone, and Evan slid out of his shorts before lowering himself to the ground, pulling Aidy down with him. She steadied herself over his lap as he held her close and kissed the tops of her breasts.

Aidy knew he wanted more than that. She pulled away from his kisses and lifted her tank top over her head. Her breasts fell free as she tossed the shirt aside. Evan cupped them and immediately began to kiss and suck, burying himself in her hold. Aidy moaned as he pulled her closer, then kissed his hair as he slowed his bites and licked and kissed her nipples. His kisses moved from her breasts to her stomach, from her stomach back up to her shoulders. Aidy felt exhilarated not just by her own desires being met, but by experiencing just how much Evan wanted her.

His desires deserved to be filled. Aidy pushed him towards the ground, kissing him as they wrapped their arms around one another. She kissed a path from his neck to his chest, and licked his nipples while she hooked her thumbs under the waistband of his briefs. She could already feel him growing hard against her hip, but she still felt a flash of shocked excitement when she pulled down his underwear and saw his erection, already large at half mast, waiting for her.

She gently massaged his cock, and he closed his eyes as he took a deep breath. Aidy took the opportunity to bend down and surprise him by replacing her palm with her tongue. Evan gasped as Aidy curled her tongue around his shaft, licking up and up to get him ready. After one last lick, she wet her lips and slid his cock into her mouth.

Evan's groan rippled through the trees. She sucked his cock and stroked it with her tongue. He seemed to like it best when she would press the tip of his cock against the roof of her mouth and lick it in rapid strokes. He stroked her hair and begged her for more. She provided, sucking and licking him as she gripped his ass with both hands.

Evan sat up as Aidy slid her mouth off of his cock. He moved towards her, and she wrapped her legs around him as he kissed her and laid her on the ground. His hands moved up her legs and to her shorts. She pulled from his kisses to allow him to easily undress her. He pulled off her shorts, then her underwear, tossing both to the side before kissing her legs. Aidy closed her eyes and readied herself to be entered by him.

Aidy felt him kiss her inner thighs. She opened her eyes just as Evan's head moved deeper between her legs. She gasped as Evan's tongue slid inside of her. He started with long, lingering strokes, each one deeper than the one before it. Aidy groaned as Evan gripped her hips and kept his head steady. His tongue stayed inside of her, moving in circles and waves. He lifted his head, but before Aidy could beg him not to stop, he gently pressed her clit with his thumb.

Aidy threw back her head and groaned even louder. She felt a rush of tingles forming in her toes. Evan pressed her clit again, then kept pressing it gently as his tongue moved back inside of her. Aidy's hips began to rock, and Evan slid his tongue in deeper and pressed her clit harder.

The tingles turned into a scream that rippled from Aidy's throat and caused her body to open like a morning glory at dawn. She lay on the ground and breathed heavily as Evan moved up from between her legs. He kissed her neck and massaged her breasts, giving her a moment to recover.

Aidy didn't need a moment. She pulled Evan close and began to kiss him, covering him with her gratitude as she wrapped her legs around him once more. She felt how hard he was, harder than he'd been in her mouth. She opened herself to him, and he slid inside of her. They both groaned upon each other's touch.

Evan began to thrust. He didn't bother to start slowly, and Aidy was grateful. She arched her back and moved her hips in time with his thrusts, relishing the friction of his cock rubbing up and down inside of her. She was so wet she was afraid he'd slip out, but Evan held her close and thrust back just enough to move, but not enough to move out. Aidy felt her body grow warm as Evan's gasps grew shorter and his thrusts became faster. His gasps became cries, and Aidy knew he was close. She wrapped her legs around his back and pulled him as deep into her as he could go.

Evan stopped. Aidy felt the warm rush of his seed, the throb of his orgasm as he gasped for air and said, "Oh God … oh God … oh …"

Aidy held Evan as he lowered himself on top of her. She closed her eyes and ran her fingers through the beads of sweat along his back. The wind in the leaves moved in time with their breath.

———

Aidy and Evan spent the rest of the day with each other. They talked, they ate, and they fucked. When one or the other was too spent to have sex, they made out. They didn't bother dressing until the sun went down and the cold night air was too much for their sweat-soaked skin. "I'll miss you being naked, though," Evan said as he pulled on his shorts.

"I'll strip down as soon as the sun comes up," Aidy promised with a grin. She was about to kiss his cheek when she saw him stare at her with frightened eyes. "What?"

Evan pointed at her hair. Aidy frowned as she combed her fingers through the strands. She felt something small and smooth fall into her palm. She looked down and saw a tiny green leaf.

"Oh, thank God," Evan said. Aidy looked back up at him. He looked much calmer than before. Still, he bowed his head. "I'm sorry," he added. "I thought you were turning into … I'd heard about people who weren't taken by the plants, but —"

"Became them?" Aidy asked.

Evan nodded, and absently brushed a cluster of seeds from his thigh. Aidy remembered what Theresa had said about Chris. She remembered the feeling she'd had about Jake. She remembered the dirt she'd scrubbed from her nails.

Evan looked back up at Aidy, his eyes sad, but looking more hopeful when they looked upon her. "What do you think people do?" he asked. "When … when they realize what they're becoming?"

Aidy sat for a moment, thinking of people wandering in the forest to become what consumed them. She shrugged. "I don't know."

"Do you think it'll happen to us?"

She examined her nails. They were dirty, but no dirtier than before. "I think it's always happened, in a way," she said. "People becoming the soil. I — I guess if I had to choose, I'd rather meet that fate than fall prey to the vines."

"Yeah." Evan chuckled with a twinge of sadness. "Yeah, I guess I would too. But it sounds like we don't have a choice."

"Probably not." She thought of the choices she'd made over the past several scratch marks on her log. The only choices that made her feel alive since the Growth were the ones she made that brought her closer to Evan. Being near him kept her going and gave her hope. Even if it only kept her going until the forest devoured her in one way or another, it was better than being cold and alone.

Aidy scooted closer to Evan, and he embraced her. "We don't know when it will happen," she whispered. She kissed him, and he held her cheek. Her skin warmed as he pulled her close and kissed her with more fervor.

Aidy pulled away and gave Evan a small smile. "But we can be animals until then."

# HE TRAPPED MY THOUGHTS INSIDE MY HEAD

He trapped my thoughts inside my head
Afraid of what they'd bring.
He worried that the pain they caused
Would find its way to him.

He held me down and tied a cord
Around my tattered mind.
He smiled as he saw that all
My words were in a bind.

But in his swiftness to ensure
My thoughts were tightly bound,
The cord was stretched too tightly
And he heard an awful sound.

I soon cried out! My thoughts burst through!
Their darkness and their tones
Lay scattered on the floor
Along with all his broken bones.

I smiled at the knowledge of
Just what my thoughts could do.
Be careful, for the pain they caused
Could find its way to you.

# A Note From the Author

Thanks for reading *Little Paranoias: Stories*! If you could please take a minute to review the book on Amazon or Goodreads, I'd really appreciate it.

# Acknowledgments

In September 2018, I received my first acceptance. I got an email saying that "Hearts are Just 'Likes,'" my social media update of "The Tell-Tale Heart," would be published along-side 29 other tales in Camden Park Press' *Quoth the Raven: A Contemporary Reimagining of the Works of Edgar Allan Poe.*

I was ecstatic when I saw the acceptance, not just because it was an acceptance, but because it was a project I wanted so much to be a part of when I first read the call for submissions. I adore Poe, and I was thrilled to have the chance to reimagine one of my favorite stories of his in the context of Instagram.

I found that call for submission in a Facebook group dedicated to open horror markers — a group I was invited to join by Sheri White.

Sheri and I were friends before I began writing. We have a mutual friend that both of us met online, and after we chatted in the comments of one of his posts, we friended each other. We realized we lived close to each other, and we met in person at the annual D.C. Tattoo Convention in January 2017.

Sheri was an established author by the time I began to write seriously in 2016. She was the editor of Morpheus Tales (still is) and had several published works in various anthologies and eZines. In the fall of 2016, I was working on *Please Give* and had completed three short stories. I was starting to think this writing thing might have legs. But I wanted someone to read my work before I started submitting it to markets. I also wanted some advice on how and where to submit. I decided to ask Sheri, hoping she'd help, but understanding if she didn't have the time.

Sheri helped. She read the earliest drafts of "The Crow's Gift" and "All the Pieces Coming Together," and invited me to join two Facebook groups dedicated to open story markets. Her help continued as my interest in writing persisted. She invited me to two "women in horror" groups, one of which is where I first saw Nina D'Arcangela's call for entries in her monthly flash picture prompt challenge (many of my entries for the challenge now appear in this collection). Sheri also invited me to join a writers group with other Maryland/DC/Virginia-based authors, and told me about various cons, including Scares That Care (she was also my ride to Scares That Care). She's read my work and reviewed it honestly online.

Sheri's been amazing, and I'm so grateful for everything she's done to help me grow as a writer. I don't just mean that in terms of getting better at storytelling or navigating through calls for submissions. She inspires me because of that helping hand. She shows me how to be an excellent mentor and friend for a fellow writer, and I do my best to emulate that when I meet fellow writers. While I'm not experienced enough to consider myself a mentor, I try to boost other authors, share opportunities, and keep up the encouragement. I try to be like Sheri, and I also try to be a good friend in kind to her.

So first and foremost, I want to acknowledge and thank Sheri White. Her friendship and help have all been valuable, and I'm glad we can chat about writing, movies, tattoos, and beer with each other.

I'd also like to thank the first editor to accept my work for publication: Lyn Worthen, the editor behind *Quoth the Raven*. The anthology is truly remarkable. I would enjoy it even if I weren't in it. The stories are all gems, which is rare — I sometimes only find a few highlights in an anthology, but

Worthen managed to find 30. Thank you, Lyn, for seeing my work as worthy enough to be included alongside these pieces.

I want to thank the editing team behind The Sirens Call, a bimonthly horror eZine: Gloria Bobrowicz, Lee A. Forman, Erin Lydia Prime, and Nina D'Arcangela. I received my first acceptance to The Sirens Call for Issue 42, and have had pieces accepted and published by their team ever since. They were also kind enough to feature me in Issue 46. I'm grateful for their work in the horror community and their kindness to indie authors like myself.

I want to give an extra shoutout to Nina, who runs a monthly flash picture challenge on her blog, Spreading the Writer's Word. The challenge keeps me writing — I can say I write at least one story or poem per month thanks to this challenge, and those add up! It also gets me out of the comfort zone of my own head, and gives me pieces I can later submit to journals (or publish in my own collections).

Thanks also to Tiffany Key, editor of Mercurial Stories, for publishing "Stick Figure Family."

Of course, I can't write an Acknowledgments essay without thanking my editor, Evelyn Duffy. She brought her amazing editor's eye to every story in this collection, including ones that had previously been published. She has helped me grow as a writer and uses her editing to not only correct and polish my work, but to help keep it growing along with my years in this field. She assures me my work is good while also pushing me to make it better, and for that, I'm grateful.

Thanks as always to Doug Puller, who formatted this book and did the amazing cover art. His work is fantastic, and I'm grateful we get to work together on these projects. My books always feel real once he's worked his magic on them!

I also want to give a special shoutout to my friend Lani Prunés. She was a beta reader for several pieces in this collection, including "Seed," "Quadrapocalypse," an early version of "Weary Bones," and "Hearts are Just 'Likes.'" She was especially helpful on "Hearts are Just 'Likes,'" for she works in social media and helped me get the finer points of the Influencer world down pat. She also gave me the idea to add more to "Weary Bones" when she expressed disappointment with how quickly it ended, leading me to expand the story into what Evelyn called a lifetime. Thanks so much, Lani. I hope we can get bubble tea again soon.

There are tons of people I've had the pleasure of meeting both online and offline, writers and bloggers and bookstagrammers who make writing and publishing an amazing experience. Thank you Erin, Steve, Tracy, Emily, Toni, Laurie, Jen, Tiffany, Loren, Sidney, Sam, Gabino, Violet, Suzie, Jamie, and many more. You all are amazing and I'm so lucky to know you.

Thanks to Mom and Dad for their continued support and encouragement. Thanks Dad for finishing *Without Condition* even though reading such graphic material from your daughter was probably tough. Thank you Mom for buying copies of my books to sell to colleagues and friends. It all means the world to me, and I'm so fortunate to have such wonderful parents.

And, last but far from least, I want to thank my husband, Will. Your encouragement, love, compassion, and strength fuel me and get me through my day-to-day much more nicely than my fears ever will. I love you.

# Previously Published Works

"Hearts are Just 'Likes'" was previously published in a slightly different form in *Quoth the Raven: A Contemporary Reimagining of the Works of Edgar Allan Poe*; from Camden Park Press.

"The Note on the Door" was previously published in a slightly different form in *The Sirens Call*, Issue 41: "Halloween Screams and Other Dark Things."

"Death is a Hunter" was previously published in a slightly different form in *The Sirens Call*, Issue 42: "The Bitter End."

"A Part of You" and "Stick Figure Family" was previously published in a slightly different form in *The Sirens Call*, Issue 43: "Women in Horror Month 10."

"Snowfall" was previously published in a slightly different form in *The Sirens Call*, Issue 44: "Can You Feel It?"

"Stick Figure Family" was previously published in a slightly different form in *Mercurial Stories*, Vol. 1, Issue 36: "Oh, the Horror."

# About the Author

Sonora Taylor is the author of *Without Condition*, *The Crow's Gift and Other Tales*, *Please Give*, and *Wither and Other Stories*. Her short story, "Hearts are Just 'Likes,'" was published in Camden Park Press' *Quoth the Raven*, an anthology of stories and poems that put a contemporary twist on the works of Edgar Allan Poe. Taylor's short stories frequently appear in *The Sirens Call*, a bi-monthly horror eZine. Her work has also appeared in *Mercurial Stories*, *Tales to Terrify*, and the *Ladies of Horror Fiction* podcast. She is currently working on her third novel. She lives in Arlington, Virginia, with her husband.

Visit Sonora online at sonorawrites.com.

CPSIA information can be obtained
at www.ICGtesting.com
Printed in the USA
LVHW091030080621
689691LV00010B/116

9 781686 625565